To my DaShawn, my Morgan, my Ernie, my Tara, my Jason, my Lis, my Derek, my Curio, and my lovely wife, Libni-

Thank You.

For Jon.

"Take your broken heart, make it into art."

-Carrie Fisher

Tracklisting

1. Big Brother (Kanye West)

I just wanna start by saying that I don't hate White people. It's Zombies that I can't stand. They arrive in large amounts and destroy everything. They cover the town like that blizzard back in '96. Brooklyn has officially been taken over, and it annoys the hell outta me.

Oh, and I don't mean actual Zombies like from The Walking Dead. Me and Bree call hipsters 'Zombies'. You've probably seen 'em. They're at the corner store trying their hardest to order a chopped cheese with finesse but are sticking out way too much.

You can hear 'em from your window waiting for their Uber to arrive and trying to figure out which bar to hit up in the city.

My room is dark, but the light from my cell phone is a constant reminder that I suck at falling asleep. I Googled it and found out that lying on your back helps but that was an hour ago. The most comforting thing about having insomnia in New York City is that you're always in earshot of an entertaining conversation just outside your window. The second most comforting thing is that every five minutes there are sounds of sirens blaring and flying down the street, reminding you that you're not the only one awake.

I don't usually pick up the phone at 2:37 am.

But it's Justine.

I mean, it's not a strange thing for me to be awake at two in the morning but ignoring phone calls at this hour is my way of passively telling people, "It's too damn late to be calling someone's phone, even if you have known them since the 8th grade."

"What do you want, Justine?"

"Lenny, what the hell is wrong with your brother?!"

"You want the complete diagnosis?" I tease.

"I'm serious, Lenny. He's a real fucked up person."

Usually, I entertain Justine's meltdowns but it's way too late, and I honestly don't have the emotional energy to play this game.

"What is it this time?" I ask as if I couldn't already guess.

"Lenny, am I stupid? He called about an hour ago talking about he needed a ride home and that he was too drunk to ride the subway. So I drive forty minutes into the city to get him from some random address he sent me, and when I text him that I'm five minutes away, he tells me to forget it because he's staying the night at Cristina's. What kinda shit is that?"

"I'm real sorry, Justine, but you let him do this kinda stuff to you all the time. You should've just told him that you couldn't go get him."

"Lenny. Why is your brother the only person blind to the fact that I freakin' love him?"

15

"I don't think he's blind. I think he's just not interested, that's all."

The truth is that my brother has a type and Justine just ain't it. If you ask me, Justine is a catch, for sure. She graduated from Howard the same year I graduated from Morehouse but is somehow doing way better in life than me or anyone else who graduated with us. For some reason, things just flowed in the perfect direction once she finished her degree in African Studies. Justine was one of those girls that went hard at everything she did. I mean, whatever she did, she gave it her all. She also made sure you knew that she was Black and damn proud of it.

When we first met in junior high school, she made sure I knew two things: that she was going to be the first Black, female president and that she was going to marry my little brother, Bree. Even though he was a grade beneath us, she had made up her mind that she would be Mrs. Justine Mitchell, by way of my knuckle-head little bro.

It made sense, too, because Bree is everything that she admires. He says what's on his mind, even when it's not very convenient. He thrives off of correcting people. Like his name, for instance. Most people assume (like any normal person) that his name, 'Brian' is pronounced Bry-Ehn. It's actually pronounced Bree-Ahn, kinda like a syllable short of the name Brianna. Our dad won't ever tell us why he and our mom decided on that weird pronunciation, but Brian made sure people got it right.

Every.

Single.

Time.

Sometime, in around the third grade or so, I made it up in my mind that I'd call him 'Bree' for short so that people got it right more often than not.

There are so many other things to know about my brother, but perhaps the most important thing to know is that he would never, ever date a Black girl. No one quite understands it, but they don't question it. And if ever they did, he'd go into full-on professor mode:

"Here's the thing..." Bree would say,

"Black girls are pretty, without a

17

doubt. I just prefer Spanish girls. It's not a race thing, it's just my preference. Now, a light-skinned Black girl MIGHT get a pass but she'd still be Black so it wouldn't really work. I'm aware that some Spanish girls can be dark-skinned, but that's okay because technically, they're not Black. Again, nothin' wrong with a Black girl. I just wouldn't date one."

Obviously, that's some pretty jacked-up logic, but no one argues with him about it because my brother is probably one of the most headstrong individuals you will ever meet. I don't think he's got a problem with Black girls. He's mostly just got a problem with hood girls[1]. But that could just be me defending him again. I mean, we hadn't had many positive, Black-woman role models to look up to where we grew up, starting with our absent mother.

---

[1] Commonly raised in urban ghettos. Often stereotyped as girls who seldom finish high school, dress inappropriately and probably don't have much of a future ahead of them.

And so back to Justine.

Calling me.

At 2 am.

In denial.

"Lenny, what should I do?"

I'm honestly in no mood to pacify Justine at this hour, so I'm gonna keep it very real with her. I explain to Justine that Bree is like Biggie[2] back in '95. Not that Bree could rap or anything, but that he was on the hunt for his light-skinned Faith Evans. I tell her that Bree wants a chick that is super pretty and could give him some light-skinned babies with good hair. I reminded Justine that she was a darker girl and that her inability to ever be light-skinned or soft-haired left her to be Bree's, Lil Kim. You guys remember Lil' Kim, right? Biggie's dark-skinned side chick that everyone knew would ride out for him but could never really land that wifey spot. I told Justine that she was Lil' Kim in Bree's world.

---

[2] Otherwise known as The Notorious B.I.G., Brooklyn rapper who is arguably the best rapper in hip-hop. He is also famous for his beef with West Coast rapper Tupac Shakur before his untimely death in March of 1997.

Harsh, but true.

"That's probably the worst analogy I've ever heard, Lenny. I'm just gonna head back home and try to get some sleep," she says.

That makes two of us tonight.

"Whatever. Goodnight, Jus."

"Night Lenny."

Even after the three beeps let me know Justine's hung up, and it's safe to go back to scrolling through Facebook, I keep the phone up to my ear. Being on the call with her made my phone warm, and it feels good against my skin. Somehow, the warmth to my face is making my whole body warm and 2 am is the hour when you'll try just about anything to fall asleep.

It used to be sex that put me to sleep, but these days it feels like it wakes me up more than anything. It's starting to get cold in New York, but my dad is too cheap to turn on the heat. He considers September to be "still summer" and refuses to put the heat on before Thanksgiving arrives.

There is this weird time between the first day of school in September and the day after Halloween when you don't really know when it's safe to pull out your North Face and take the AC out of the window. During this time in NYC, it could be as warm as Florida one day and then cold and wet like Seattle on the next. I've never been to either of those places, but I know what the weather is like there. Sometimes I open the weather app on my phone and type in the names of cities that I've never been to. Places like Greece and San Diego. I think it's pretty dope that you can know what kind of clothes the weather calls for at any moment in places that are miles away from you.

I guess I can't be too mad at Justine for being such a sucker for my brother. The truth is that I'm probably the biggest sucker of them all. Bree feels more like a kid to me than he does a kid brother. Our mom left before either of us could see enough of her face to remember what she looked like. Me and Bree suppose that her leaving is what turned my dad into a robot. We call him that because he's here, but he's got no feelings.

About anything.

Some days I'll say, "Hey dad, you want me to pray for you?" His response is always, "Just pray for the world, son." He's always been that way. We've never gone a night without a hot meal, and there's never been a leaky drain in this entire three-story brownstone. Honestly, I'd trade a meal and a tight faucet for a hug from my father on any day. Me and Bree have kinda accepted that it's just the way he is and that some other kids have it way worse. And if we ever forgot for a second that we have it better than most kids, my dad was sure to remind us.

'This brownstone is one of the last on this whole block! Y'all let these yuppies come in and buy everything out but not me. And y'all better not sell it once I'm dead. I worked my ass off since I was twenty-two to pay off this house and my grandkids will own it. Everybody else can sell but not us, you hear me? It's bad enough they drivin' up the prices on everything from gas to groceries

22

over here because of them hip-stars or whatever the hell y'all call 'em. Don't sell this damn house! This is the Mitchell home. I worked too damn hard..."

The bit never changes. Sometimes, me and Bree can mimic him word for word once he gets going — with our backs turned, of course.

So that's:

1. no mom and

2. a robot for a dad, which makes me Bree's dad.

Sorta.

We used to get teased about it all the time. Bree would fall asleep on me on the bus because he gets motion sickness, even when we were too old. I never really minded it unless the kids from the neighborhood were around. I don't know how things are wherever you grew up, but there were just some things you didn't do in Brooklyn. Bree followed me everywhere I went, which was cool because we're pretty close in age, but he was always doing weird shit. Like calling me 'Papi'.

"Bree, you gotta stop calling me papi.
That shit is gay and people think it's weird."

　　　　"It's not gay, it's a term of endearment."

"No. It's what Spanish chicks call either
their dads or the nigga knockin' their
socks off. It's weird."

　　　　"Nigga, you papi. That's it."

Sometimes he'll shorten it and just call me "pap" (p-ah-p). I hated it, but after a while, it wasn't so weird. Other people got used to it too. It still freaks people out from time to time if they've never really been around us. I'm not stupid, though. Bree's got daddy issues, and so do I.

So I teach him how to fill out financial aid online, and he goes, "thanks, pap."

It works.

It's 4 am now and my phone is ringing.

Justine again?

Of course not.

The caller I.D. reads, Baby Bro.

There is no feeling like the mini panic attack I have whenever he calls.

"Yooooo! Papi, you was sleep?"

"Was I <u>asleep</u>? The answer is no. Why what's up?" I ask him.

"Don't try and play me, nigga. I need a favor," he says.

"It's 4 am, Bree. What could you possibly need, a condom?"

"Funny, but no. I need you to come meet me at Myrtle train station in like thirty or forty minutes. Please don't say no. You're already up and I know you ain't doing shit but lookin' at Facebook."

"Bree, you're the only person that I know who asks for favors like this. Why didn't you just take the ride from Justine when she came to get you?"

"Damn. I knew she would call you. I'll tell you about it when I get to the train station. Meet me there, nigga. Myrtle Ave., don't be late!"

"Nigga, wait," I yell.

"What?"

"You're coming on the J train or the G?" I ask.

"The G," he says. "I'm coming from Wash Heights, and the A is still running express, so I'll be there in no time."

He's lying. The trains stopped running express hours ago. He knows that. And I know that too, but it won't stop me from picking him up.

"Why do you need me to come get you then? The G train is only two blocks away."

"Oh... Cuz I forgot my key, and I need you to let me in," he tells me.

"Bruh. Are you serious? Just call me when you get here!"

"Nah, I need you to come and get me, please pap? Just be there. Forty minutes, tops. Thank yooooou!"

He hung up.

And he sounds drunk.

Why is it that when a situation pops up, the urge to fall asleep decides to suddenly show up? I guess I don't really have a choice. It's been about thirty minutes since Bree hung up on me and chances are, he's waiting by the turnstile in the station because he doesn't wanna wait for me outside. I don't care how long you've been living here, everyone knows that you don't stand still in Bedstuy. Or in any part of Brooklyn, for that matter. You've gotta be coming or going, but you NEVER stand still. It practically screams: I'm not from around here, please rob me!

I throw on the basketball shorts that were already on the floor by my bed and grabbed a tank top from the top drawer on the way out of my room.

Sneakers or slippers?

I go for the Nike slippers.

Keys.

Phone.

Chapstick.

Wallet.

I take my time getting out of the house. The train station is only two blocks away, but I wanna show Bree how much of a dick he is for making me get out of my bed this late.

"Too scared to wait for me on the corner?" I teased him as I make my way down into the station.

"Whatever, Lenny. Yo' ass woulda did the same thing," he shouted back.

We share a laugh and then make our way up the steps and back toward Bedford Avenue. I don't feel inconvenienced at all, but I can't let him know that. I secretly enjoy being someone he can rely on because there aren't many things left to love in Brooklyn. If you love a friend, drugs or a bullet might take 'em away. If you love a barbershop or West-Indian restaurant, the hipsters come and buy it out so that they can squeeze a set of condos in its place. So for the last twenty-seven years, I've been teaching myself how to keep from loving things. Bree's all that I have left to love.

"You think the pizza shop on Franklin is open right now?" Bree asks.

"We're not stopping for pizza, Bree. Plus, that's out of our way. I'm going home."

"Wow. So you're gonna let me starve?"

"You're twenty-six years old. You let yourself starve if you didn't eat at whoever's house you were just at. Was it Cristina?"

"Whatever, yo. Justine has a big ass mouth."

"And a big ass heart," I add. "Why you always playin' her, Bree?"

"I'm not always playin' her. She plays herself. She knows I'm not feelin' her like that, but she constantly makes herself available. So, if she wants to be my emergency contact, I'm not gonna stop her."

"You're a trip," I tell him.

I stand by my opinion that Justine and Bree would make some beautiful, Black, opinionated babies. Bree definitely got all the prettiness from our mom. There are no pictures in the house of her and pops never really talks about her. But when I look at Bree, I know she had to be beautiful. Bree wears his hair

29

short, not much longer than a dark caesar-cut. But when he does let it grow for too long, you can tell that it's soft and light brown. My hair is thick and dark. I actually prefer it that way because I can grow it into a high-top fade. Not too high, like the Fresh Prince, but high enough to remind the Zombies that I been living here before them.

We turn the corner onto our block, and the cops are arresting someone just steps away from our stoop. A few people are surrounding the scene with their cell phones out, but some officers are backing them away from whatever is going on. I think there's a female screaming, "Let him go!"

"Oh snap, they got somebody," Bree shouted.

"I didn't see anything when I left the house to pick you up from the train. This must've just happened. Don't even look, just keep going."

"You don't wanna see what's going on?" he asks.

"No, Bree. Let's just mind our business."

What doesn't make sense to me is why my dad won't move us out of this neighborhood. He's got way too much pride in this run-down Brownstone. We live right across the street from the projects, and sometimes it feels like the only difference between us and them is that we pay for water and electricity.

We both walk through the gate to our house while still looking to see what's going on a few houses down. The blue and red lights are flashing, so it makes it hard to see who the cops are arresting. The truth is that I do wanna see what's going on but it's not worth becoming the next hashtag. Whoever they're arresting, I guarantee you it's not a Zombie. Zombies always get a free pass. If a zombie is caught drinking alcohol outside, they get a warning and possibly a ride home. One of us gets caught outside with an open beer bottle, it's two warning shots to the face.

Me and Bree go through the first-floor entrance because it's easier to sneak in without waking our dad that way. Bree lives on the bottom level, and I live at the top. My dad lives on the second floor, so we never go in that way. The keys aren't even the same. I can't even tell you what the second floor of our walk-up looks like anymore, besides the hallways that we pass on our way up and down. It's pretty annoying having to come in through the ground floor when I'm all the way up on the third floor, but my father likes his privacy. I guess we all kinda prefer our own space. It wasn't always this way, though.

In order to pay this place off, there used to be tenants living with us all the time. Some people stayed for a few months, and other people stayed for years. When I left for college, my father made it clear that he wanted me to come back and live at the house. I don't know why but it was almost a condition for me to be able to go to Georgia for school. I've never heard my dad say that he loved me or that he missed me but him making me promise to come back and live in Brooklyn was kinda like having both of those things wrapped up in one request. When I got back last year, he broke the news to me and Bree that he wasn't renting out the rooms anymore and that he wanted us to occupy the house. Each of us got a floor. Bree chose the bottom, and so I got stuck at the top. Closer to the stars, I guess.

"Hey, I think that was Officer James arresting that dude outside. Maybe you can find out what happened tomorrow?" Bree asks.

"Why me? You ask him, nosey."

"He comes into your coffee shop every morning, pap. Find out what happened."

"Alright, I'll ask him tomorrow. I'm heading upstairs, though."

"Aight, don't wake daddy on the way up. We'll never hear the end of it."

"You're not even lyin'. I'll see you in the morning, Bree."

"Alright. Love you, pap."

"Love you too, bro."

"Don't call me that," he says.

"My bad, bro," I joke.

He flips me the bird.

Bree hated when I called him 'bro'. When the Zombies started moving in, it's all you would hear them say.

"Oh, bro! Check out this dope thing I discovered at this place in Bushwick[3]. It's like super cheap and super good. I bet no one knows about this! Let's call our other bros and be bros about this cool bro that we just bro'd. Broooooo!"

Bree couldn't stand it. One time, he spent an hour telling me about how that's their word and that even though he and I were bros, I'd better not ever actually call him bro. So I do it anyway just to get under his skin.

It's 4:43 am.

I make it past my dad's floor and head up to my own. I peel out of my clothes and fall into bed all in one swift motion. I can hear my dad's alarm go off and I know he'll be getting up for work soon. Bree is on the first floor probably in his third dream already, and finally, sleep has begun to find me. The red and blue

---

[3] Commonly referred to now as *"East Williamsburg"* but do NOT believe that shit. Bushwick is a neighborhood that runs through Brooklyn and Queens and is the land of some of the dopest barber shops, 2am food spots and clothing stores, run predominantly by Hispanics.

lights outside are piercing through my closed eyelids. I don't know who's getting arrested this time, but I'm just glad it ain't Bree.

One last text comes through before I completely pass out. It's Bree asking if I remembered to take my pill.

I hadn't.

2. "Candy Shop" (50 Cent ft. Olivia)

I woke up this morning to the sound of rocks being thrown at my window. In 2017, someone is throwing rocks at my friggin' window. I check my phone, and it's 8:17 in the morning.

It's Saturday.

Shit!

Alexis.

Four missed calls.

I jump outta the bed and lift up the window. Alexis is waiting on the sidewalk just outside my window with a hand full of pebbles, ready to chuck another if I hadn't yelled at him.

"Alexis, I overslept bro. I'll throw you the keys now!"

Alexis is this sixteen-year-old Dominican kid from Ridgewood[4]. He rides his bike about twenty blocks every morning to help out at my coffee shop. He's too young to be put on payroll, but I slide him fifty dollars a day off the books. The truth is, he's more of a liability than he is a help, but it keeps him off the streets for the summer.

And I'm also kinda dating his sister.

On and off, I guess.

We're off right now, thanks to Bree. Last week, he logged onto Facebook and commented on a picture of me and Lisaura saying:

---

[4] Neighborhood in Queens that borders Brooklyn. Popular attractions include the Ridgewood theatre and *Fleur de Lis*, a catering hall where everybody and they momma had their Junior High school prom celebration. Both attractions are gone now.

"Wow, you two look cute together. Are those her two kids? Nice. Maybe if she woulda swallowed, you guys could start your own family and you wouldn't be their stepdad. #goals"

Thankfully, I had only gotten three texts from mutual friends telling me that I'd better "check Facebook, quick!" I was able to delete the comment in time. I wasn't able to keep Lisaura from buggin' out on me, though.

"Your brother is a fucking angel in your eyes! He can't do anything wrong, according to you. Why would he think that I would find that funny? And you not gonna check him? Fine, I'm out! Good luck finding ANYBODY that's gonna put up with him. I love you but clearly, you love your brother more. Maybe you two should go get married or some shit."

Lisaura wasn't wrong. My brother tends to take things too far. That was last week. I ask Alexis every day to have his sister call me so we can talk. I've even been slipping him an extra twenty dollars a day hoping that she'd think it was sweet and reach out to me. I know they need all the help they can get in that house.

But back to Alexis.

Outside.

Waiting for the keys to the shop.

"Alexis," I shout. "Open the gate but leave it halfway down so they know we're not open yet."

"Okay, got it Mr. Mitchell!" he yells back.

"I told you, you can call me Lenny. You know me, Alexis."

"Okay, sorry Lenny."

"It's alright. Remember to empty the urns that are soaking from last night, wash them one more time and then start brewing the new coffee."

"Okay," he yells again.

"Oh, and don't tie your bike up out front. You gotta put it in the garden out back now, got it?"

"Okay Mr. Mi-, I mean. Okay Lenny," he corrects himself.

"Dope. I'll be down in thirty minutes but if I'm not, lift the gate and have Officer James' coffee ready and apologize to him about us opening late today."

"Okay, but Lenny?"

"What, Alexis?!"

"I need the keys," he says with a smirk, showing his chipped tooth.

"Right! Sorry, bro. Hold on."

I run to the kitchen and grab the keys to the shop off of the wall-hook and then run back down the hall to my bedroom. I lean out and launch the keys at Alexis, who catches them and obviously should be taking up baseball instead of working at my coffee shop.

Just then, my dad poked his head out of the second-floor window.

"I know y'all better stop yelling outta this goddamn window!"

"Alexis, just go. I'll be down, ASAP," I yell one more time.

I can hear my dad making his way up the stairs. Thirteen creaky steps separate my space from his space. Then again, if you ask him, this whole house is his space.

"Let me be clear: This is MY house. Y'all two knuckleheads get to stay here. Everything in here is mine. These are my floors and my walls. Remember that. If you don't like it, my door swings both ways."

That's just another one of his speeches that Bree and I know word for word. What's funny is that if either of us ever really did try to leave, we'd get a whole 'nother speech about how we're family and how family has to stick together.

He walks into my bedroom just as I get done brushing my teeth. I step into the shower right as he pokes his head into the bathroom. I really/ don't want to hear a lecture about how yelling out the window is 'ghetto'.

"I'm naked, you know," I tell him, jokingly.

"Yeah well I diapered it for three years, so I think I'd know what it looks like."

"I guarantee you a lot has changed since then, pop."

"Yeah, yeah. Spare me the details. I see you and your knucklehead brother don't know what a decent time to be in the house is. It's bad enough the cops out here shootin' folks left and right. Y'all asses don't need to be outside at no four in the damn morning."

"We only stepped out for just a second, dad. Bree wanted pizza so we went."

"Bullshit. Justine called me this morning and told me about what your brother did last night. Damn shame what y'all two do to that poor girl."

"Not me, dad. Bree. Do you mind, though? It's kinda hard talking to you and washing my balls at the same time."

"Hey, now! Show me some respect and don't be talkin' about your balls in front of me."

"Sorry," I say.

I wasn't really sorry. All I want is for him to leave. Plus, he only ever wants us to be nice to Justine because her dad is rich. That's just like my dad to be protecting relationships that involve money.

"Where you rushing off to anyway, that damn candy shop?"

"It's not a candy shop," I say "It's a coffee shop, dad."

"I thought you said it was a candy shop," he says.

"It was a candy shop when I bought it. Now it's a coffee shop."

"Oh, well how am I supposed to know what it is? I don't know why you tryna sell coffee to the folks in this neighborhood anyway. We don't need no coffee shops. You shoulda put a check cashing place or something. Now that's what we need."

"Dad, why would I put a check cashing place here? It'd be better to open a bank or something."

"Now why would you open a bank?" he asks. "Why would people use banks when you can just cash your checks and have your money in your hand?

43

Banks are useless. What, I'm gonna pay someone to hold my money for me and then have them tell me when I can take it out? Hell nah."

"It's not about that, pops. It's about saving your money and investing it and allowing it to grow and stuff."

"No way, son. I can save my own money. My bank is my pillowcase. Whenever I need to make a withdrawal, I just lift up my head and take out what I need."

"You got it, pops. Whatever you say. I kinda need to get to work now so could you leave so I can get outta the shower?"

"I don't know why you rushing. You the boss!" he says sarcastically.

"Yeah but I'm interviewing somebody today, and Officer James is probably already there, waiting for his morning coffee."

"Oh yeah! Make sure you ask him what was going on at four o'clock in the morning. They got somebody last night. I wonder who it was. I was peeking through the window, but I couldn't see."

"You know the apple doesn't fall too far from the tree," I say. "You and Bree are probably the nosiest people in the world."

"And you're the latest person in the world. Get to work, boss-man," he shot back.

I step out of the shower just as soon as I can hear him walking back down the stairs. I know he's my dad, but I just don't like him being in my space. Not just him, anyone really. I just think it's weird for people to see you in vulnerable moments like in the middle of a haircut or while you're still picking out clothes from the closet. Things should only be seen once they're finished and presentable.

That's just my opinion.

My feet hit the rug outside the shower, and I press them in deep to get 'em as dry as I can. I grab my towel from the rack and wrap it around my waist.

One benefit to having the whole third floor to myself is that I don't really need to leave it for anything. My bathroom is right off of my bedroom. From my bedroom, I can open up two sliding doors, and there is my living room. If I walk through my living room, I hit the kitchen, which has windows that let in the Sun and the smells from the backyard. And if I want to entertain a lady friend without having her all in my space, I can walk her in and out through the outside hallway without her seeing more than the bedroom. It's why brownstones are the best, in my opinion. They're as open or closed as you want them to be. I don't think I'd wanna live anyplace else. Brownstones keep everything in its place.

I like that.

It's not long before I'm skipping steps, headed for the front door. I've decided that today's work uniform will be a black crew neck, beige joggers, and these white Adidas that Bree says are dogged, and I need to get rid of. They're comfy, and I like 'em.

I'm usually on time for things, especially work but it probably doesn't help that my shop is directly across the street from where I live. Some people would kill to live across the street from their job, but unfortunately, it only makes me think that I've got more time than I actually do.

By the time I'm walking out of my front door, I can see from across the street that Alexis has done exactly what I've asked him to do. The gate is halfway up, which I'm realizing makes us look like the lazy business on the block. From left to right, there's an old empty lot on the corner, then a beauty salon next to it. Next to the beauty salon is my shop, then a check-cashing place, and then a bodega[5] on the corner.

I honestly don't even know how I came to own a coffee shop. Last year, I got back from school in July and found out they were selling Katy's Candy Store. That's what my coffee shop used to be. When we were kids, Katy's is where you went before and after school. Before school, you took a dollar and went and got a pack of twenty-five cent sunflower seeds, and then seventy-five cents worth of penny candies. Each day was different. If you were smart, you'd save at least one quarter to come back and play whoever was on the Marvel versus Capcom arcade game after school.

---

[5] Corner store in the hood, typically owned by Hispanics. Commonly built with bright yellow awnings decorated with colorful bulbs along the edge. Before the Arabs began dominating the corner store business, you got everything you needed form the bodega.

Katy's was the last place in the neighborhood that even had arcade games. She had a really bad cough because she smoked like a chimney. All the grown-ups would tell us not to go there because she picked out our candies with the same hand she would hack up her lung into, but Katy's candy was the best and the cheapest.

On Mother's Day, I would buy one hundred heart-shaped candies. They were the same as Swedish Fish candies, but the fact that they were heart-shaped somehow made them better. I would always ask Ms. Katy to put fifty heart candies in one bag for me and the other fifty in a bag for Bree. We liked to imagine that our mom would get jealous of all the other moms and maybe come back home on Mother's Day, and so we never wanted to be unprepared without a gift for her. The year we met Justine in junior high school, Bree took his bag and ate the candy from it. When I asked him why he said,

"She's not coming back, Lenny. Let that shit go."

I think that was the first time I hated Bree. Ms. Katy also had this parrot that was always plucking at itself and losing feathers. Now that I think of it, I'm pretty sure that bird was sick. Anyways, that parrot was our favorite. We'd all run in after school and teach it how to say stuff like, "Polly want a cracker," and "The Rock says, know your role and shut your mouth!"

Katy must not have been able to keep up with rent or something because I looked out my window last July and saw a FOR SALE sign. Bree told me that she went out of business a few months before I got back. Apparently, the whole neighborhood showed up and threw Katy a going away block party. Bree says she gave all her candy away and that no one cried. There were just a lot of laughs and free food and music.

It sucked to see Katy go out of business. Not just because we loved her so much but because we knew it wouldn't be long before a set of condos or a juice bar took its place. I mean, a coffee shop is no better but at least I own it, you know? No hipster from the outside came in and took it over. I feel like I saved one.

It kinda feels like 9/11 all over again, every time a building goes down around here. That sounds like a stretch, but it's not. Picture this: these foreigners come in and knock down buildings that you grew up staring at from your window. Everyone talks about it and are sad at first. Then it becomes a gaping hole in the ground until people aren't talking about it anymore and then they put up something pretty. Soon, no one is talking about what used to be there, and everyone is excited about the new building taking its place. The truth is, nothing will ever be like the buildings that were there before, and then you realize that you didn't take enough pictures of 'em.

But back to me.

Owning this building.

Justine's dad made some calls down to the city officials and suddenly, there was no red tape or waiting for building permits. He's an important figure in Brooklyn. He knew what Katy's shop meant to the neighborhood, and they trusted that I would honor her legacy. She needed to retire, anyway. Katy constantly complained about how there was no good coffee in

Brooklyn. So now I sell coffee out of a place I named the 'Candy Shop'. It's pretty confusing when you look it up online, but everyone in the hood gets it. Some people still even call it Katy's.

I step off the curb and slow jog across the street. The Sun is out, but the air is cold on my arms like when you step out of the shower and into an air-conditioned room. We don't open until 9 am, but I always open the shop up at 8:15 every morning for one person.

Officer James.

I duck down under the gate and push the front door open. Alexis must've gotten right to work because the front lobby is super clean. The couches on the right of the lobby are neat, and the high tables on the left of the shop are already set up for the day. The bar stretches across the entire back wall, and Alexis put all the stools out without me even having to remind him today.

"Well, well. Look who decided to show up," Mr. James said as he stood to greet me.

Officer James gets a kick out of reminding me when I'm late for our morning meetings. They're not even official meetings. We just started doing them outta nowhere when I opened the shop ten months ago. When I first opened, he just decided to show up every morning before his shift so we could talk about what was new. He was glad that I decided to buy the shop. He'd give me free advice, and I'd give him free coffee.

"I'm sorry Officer James. I must've slept through my alarm this morning. Did Alexis already get you your coffee?"

"It's fine, son," he says in a fatherly way. "Have a seat and gather yourself. How are you this morning?"

"I'm fine, I guess. I didn't really sleep well last night. I'll be alright, though. Once the afternoon rush comes around, I won't even feel like I need sleep."

"Oh, you'll be alright," he says. "When I was your age, I didn't sleep but four hours every night. There was money to be made, and you either got up to make it, or you slept in like a lazy bum. Ask your father, he knows what I'm talkin' 'bout"

"I'm sure he does," I say with a laugh. "Aye, I saw there were a few cop cars on the block early this morning. What happened?"

"Lenny, you know I can't talk about police business with you. Especially with that kid you got helping you out around here."

Just then, we hear Alexis drop something from behind the bar in the kitchen. I jump up and swing around the bar. Alexis pops his head through the rectangle cut out that connects the bar and the kitchen and reassures us that everything is okay.

"Sorry, Lenny! Nothing broke, I just thought I saw a mouse. It was only a cockroach. My bad."

"You're fine, Alexis. You need me to help you pick all this up?"

"No, it's okay," he assures me.

"Oh, Alexis," I whisper a bit. "Your sister say anything to you about me?"

"Nah, she didn't."

"You sure?" I ask him, almost hoping he'd have a different answer this time.

"I'm sure, Lenny. She ain't been sayin' nothin' about you."

"Damn... And there ain't been no new niggas at your house, right? She not talkin' to none of them niggas from Bushwick or Ridgewood?"

"Nah, she not. I know it," he says.

"Okay, cool."

I whip back around the bar in time to notice Officer James as he's finishing his coffee and grabbing his hat.

"Leaving already?" I ask.

"Well it is 8:45 and you were late this morning. Besides, you gotta get ready to open this joint up. Ms. Doris will be in here as soon as you flip that OPEN sign around and you know she don't like waiting for her coffee."

He was right.

"Alright, let's catch up tomorrow, Officer James."

I never understood Mr. James and how he could be a police officer. I mean, it made sense when I was a kid. His kids were my friends, and we never gave them a hard time about it. But now, seeing a Black man in that uniform just seems so off to me. Doesn't he see what's been going on in the news? I wanna ask him, but I don't know how rude it is to ask a question like that. This guy's job is to arrest people we know. It's crazy when you think about it.

As Officer James makes his way out of the shop, Bree is on his way in with Gabriel, one of his lame ass friends that I can't stand. Bree lifts the gate completely and turns the OPEN sign over for me.

"Nope. No, no, no, get the hell out and take Gabe with you," I tell them with my hand pointed at the door.

"Papi, why you wildin'? I just wanna ask you one question, real quick."

"No, Bree. No free coffee and there ain't no pastries left over from last night," I tell him.

"Nah, we don't want anything," he assures me. "And it's: 'there aren't any' pastries from last night. Dumb nigga."

Every now and again, Bree and I decide to talk like educated human beings. It's not often that we hold each other to such high linguistic standards— just when we feel like annoying one another.

"Whatever, just get out. Out, or throw some aprons on and help out. You know I need it," I tell them both.

"Nah, we can't help today. Just please tell this nigga Gabe that Drake is in the top five."

"Dead or alive, though?" Gabe interrupts.

"Yes, nigga! And shut up and let Lenny talk. G'head, pap. Top five best rappers, dead or alive. Drake is in there, yes?"

"I gotta agree, he's in there," I tell them. "Probably not in that number one spot but he's definitely top five."

"THANK YOU!" Bree shouts.

"Okay, then who's in your top five, cuz that's just crazy." Gabe couldn't just let it go. I guess I had a few seconds to school this chump.

"Alright, Gabriel. Bear in mind that your favorite rapper is NOT the same thing as the best rapper. If we're talking favorites, my top five is Drake, J. Cole, Jay Z, Big Sean, and Kanye West."

"In that order?!" Gabe shouts.

"Yup," I tell him. "But that's just my preference. Obviously, if we're talking financial status or greatest success story, the list changes and Jay is in the top spot. The truth is that we can't base top five, dead or alive on just finances."

"Why not?" Gabe asks.

"Well," I continue, "Cuz then dudes like KRS, Nas, and Andre 3000 don't really compete, even though they nice. They probably not broke but they not as rich as Hov[6]. Popularity changes the list too. It puts Drake at number one, but that's also just for right now because popularity changes. Listen to 'A Star is Born' by Hov and understand what I'm talkin' about. Every couple years, a different artist has the charts on smash. So if we're talking just lyrics and ability to body a track, my top five is Drake, Hov, Andre 3000, J. Cole, and Eminem."

"No Biggie??" Gabe shouts again.

"No Biggie," I assure him.

"How you from Brooklyn and Biggie not in your lyrical top five?" he asks.

---

6 *Hov* or *Hova* is another nickname for Jay Z. *Hov* is short for Jehovah. Jay Z dubbed himself "God MC" during his 2001 rap feud between him and Queens rapper, Nas.

I look at Bree, and he looks at me with a smile. We'd been through this before. Bree knew that he'd soon be dragging his friend out of my shop, kicking and screaming in disbelief.

"Gabriel, if you really go back and break down Biggie's bars, you'll see that he wasn't saying anything profound. He wasn't super conscious, and his lyrics didn't really have depth to 'em. He made hits for the ladies and dope songs talking about where he grew up. But that's it," I tell him.

"Yeah but Drake makes songs for the ladies too," Gabe interjects.

"True, but Drake also gives us bars every now and then," Bree interrupts this time.

"Even after the whole Quentin Miller thing[7], you still gon' give Drake lyrical credit?" Gabe asks in disbelief.

"Yep," I tell him confidently. "Those reference tracks are only a spectacle of what we know happens

---

[7] On July 21st, 2015, rapper Meek Mill took to Twitter accusing rapper Drake of not writing his own raps. Soon after, several reference tracks of popular Drake songs were leaked to the public. It was later learned that the reference tracks were recorded by an up and coming rapper/singer named Quentin Miller.

in studios of every one of our favorite rappers. I guarantee you that your favorite rapper has a few guys in the studio with ideas and suggestions as they record. Drake's only downfall was having been put out on front street for everyone to see."

"Yeah, but Drake is gay, yo," Gabe says.

I take a breath before responding.

"Gabriel," I say calmly. "You're obviously running out of arguable points, but I'll entertain your previous accusation. If Drake is gay for singing on tracks, then what would you call Biggie who once stated on a song that a girl looked so good that he would suck her daddy's dick?"

Gabe was quiet then.

"I thought so, ha-ha!"

Bree laughs with me.

"I don't care what you say," Gabe insists, "Biggie died as one of the greatest."

"I don't know," I tell him. "The truth is he died young, and people hold him to this greatness that he COULD have been, not the greatness that he ever actually lived to be. And that's the problem. Whenever someone dies young, we automatically deem them great when really, it's just unfortunate that they died so soon. Dying while in your prime is not the same as dying as a great."

"Not the same," Bree chimed in.

"Tupac died too soon and was great," I continue. "Amy Winehouse died too soon and was great. Biggie died too soon, but he was just alright, in my opinion."

"Bree, your brother is smoking crack, and I'm never buying anything from this bum-ass coffee shop ever again," Gabe says as he walks away.

"That's okay," I shout after him. "All you do is come around here asking for free shit anyway. Have a nice day, fellas."

Bree and his friend Gabe leave, but I'm pretty sure they'll be back asking about something else that they won't be able to settle amongst themselves. The truth is, I love Biggie. He's the best part of being from

Brooklyn, in my opinion. The first song I ever memorized was 'Juicy'.

"Oh wait, Bree!" I yell.

He hadn't made it far before he whipped around and swung the shop door back open.

"Where y'all going today?" I ask him.

"We meeting up with these two chicks from Coney Island[8]," he says with that smirk that he only does when he's about to do something stupid.

"Could you help out just for a few hours? I'm interviewing a new girl today, and I can't leave Alexis to handle the bar and the register by himself."

"You serious, pap?" he asks.

"Yo, I need you, Bree. Only for a few hours, please? I'll pay you."

"Nah, you good. What you want me to do?"

"My nigga..." I say with a smile, in my best Denzel Washington impression.

---

[8] Neighborhood in Brooklyn made popular because of its attractions, games and food. Infamous attractions include the Cyclone, the Parachute Jump, the WONDER WHEEL and Nathan's. As it is part of the lower, southwestern part of the borough, it requires a long-ass F train ride if you are traveling from the Bedford-Stuyvesant neighborhood.

Bree got right to work with almost no direction from me. He's honestly a really hard worker, and I offer him to work here with me all the time. Told him I'd even put him in charge and that I would just handle the business side of things. Bree's got an eye for putting things together, and he's always got his ear to the streets, so he knows what's hot and what's not. He turns me down whenever I ask, though. It sucks because everybody loves him when he's not being a jerk.

Despite the shitty things he said about Lisaura, Alexis likes him a lot. He treats Alexis like he's our brother too. I overhear him all the time, teaching Alexis proper English and what to say to girls on the street. I don't understand what his problem with Lisaura is. She's the sweetest girl. I know she's the reason I haven't been sleeping. It's funny how you can't remember what you did with your time before a person entered your life.

Lisaura's lips taste like the acoustic guitar intro to "Human Nature". She'd press her full lips on mine, and I would be four years old again, staring at murals of Michael Jackson on the lower east side of Manhattan while holding my father's hand.

Lisaura fit in my arms perfectly, kinda like the first time your left thumb combined the down, diagonal, forward' buttons with your right thumb on the 'square' button of a PlayStation controller to complete your first Hadoken[9]. And every time I held her after, it became a combination my hands never forgot. I could perfect that shit with my eyes closed.

Her skin is smooth, like the silk robes in TLC's "Creep" video, and her hair is the color of brown sugar. The kind that's good for you. She never dyed it. It is as innocent as it was in her baby pictures. Actually, every part of her seems untouched. Even after two kids, it's like her breasts have never been fuller, legs never more firm. Obviously, someone has loved her before me, but it's like she's always been mine.

Lisaura can't sing, but she does it anyway. And it's loud and strong like Hispanic women do. And when

---

[9] The *down, diagonal, forward, punch* combo is a famous button combination for Capcom's Street Fighter character Ryu. The *Hadoken* is a special move that allowed the character to release a force of energy at his opponent. Street Fighter is a popular arcade game released in August of 1987.

she gets to singing, she doesn't care how it sounds; she just does it with everything she has in her. All the pain and happiness and sadness put together. Her lips become tight and pursed like Selena's[10] and she mimics salsa dance moves on her own whenever I don't get up to dance with her to Marc Anthony songs.

I try really hard sometimes, but I can't explain what it's like to be away from her now. It's like someone reached into my heart and took away the feeling you get when you hear Seal's "Kiss from a Rose".

And she's so strong. Stronger than any woman I'd ever met. Nothing could break her spirit. She's a good mom and a great lover. She's the type to grab you a beer without you having to ask. She was more concerned with my dreams than her own. She knew when I needed a hug and when I needed space.

She knows about Travis Simmons and how he molested me when I was twelve, and she didn't laugh when I cried after telling her. In fact, she cried with me,

---

[10] Mexican-American mega star from the 90's, portrayed by J-Lo in a biopic. Another star that died too soon.

and she swore that she hated him more than I did, even without her knowing him.

I love her like I've never loved anyone else. I think I love her with the love of everything that's ever meant anything to me at all. Does that make sense? The only problem is that Bree hates her. And it's always been like a rule with me and him. If one of us didn't approve of a girl, she couldn't ever be family. No matter what.

"Pap!"

"Pap!" I hear again, as I come to. I must've been thinking way too hard about Lisaura because now Bree is over my shoulder.

Pointing at the door.

"Look," he says as if he saw a ghost.

Close.

It's a Zombie.

3. "Who's That Girl" (Eve)

Bree grabs me by the arm and pulls me toward the bar, away from the obviously lost girl in the doorway.

"You know that chick?" he asks.

"No," I say. "You?"

"Nigga, I just asked you if you knew her because I don't know her. Dummy."

"Right," I say, more sure this time.

"I'm here for the interview," she interrupted.

I guess Bree and I wouldn't exactly win at a whispering contest.

"Oh!" I say, trying to recover from the weird way me and Bree cut away for a quick sidebar. "Um, my name is Lenny. I own the shop. Why don't we talk in my office in the back?"

Okay, let me explain. It's not like we've never seen a White person before. It's New York City, for crying out loud. If there's a walk of life, you'll find it here. But seeing that girl in the doorway asking about a job here was like seeing a Black dude behind the counter at the Chinese spot. It's like seeing an Asian man throwing up dough behind the counter at Mike's Pizzeria. Now granted, the dudes behind the counter at Mike's are Mexican but them niggas make good pizza. You get what I'm saying?

My problem is with Zombies. They come in and change stuff. They're always in the way. They "discover" old shit and slap a new sticker on it. They go around with their little flags and stick 'em in mounds that don't belong to them. So when the girl who called yesterday about coming in for an interview is staring at me with blue jeans, black shoes, blonde hair, and white skin, me and Bree aren't exactly excited.

This girl was probably looking for the Starbucks down on Union and Grand. No way did she mean to walk in here for a job interview. I'm not discriminative, even though most people think that HBCU graduates are. I just know the rules of New York City. If I hired a White girl in here, them niggas from Marcy projects would be in here ready to eat this girl alive. But I'll entertain the poor girl.

"Have a seat," I tell her. "So you're here for a job interview, huh?"

"Yep," she assures me with a smile.

"You have a résumé with you?"

She pulls a résumé out of her bag that is bound by a bright red sliding bar and protected on both sides with clear covers. She hands it to me and sits back in her chair. Her swift movements cause a waft of air to come my way, and I can tell even from here that she smelled sweet, like something made with apples. Even though I was already preparing to deny this girl a job, I glance over her résumé.

Sara.

Penn State.

Seeking part-time work in Brooklyn.

"Sara, right?"

"Yes sir," she answers.

"You don't have to call me sir. We look about the same age," I joke with her.

"That may be true but does my age make you less of a sir?"

"I guess it doesn't," I tell her. "So how did you hear about this place?"

She explained that she had recently moved here from Iowa and that she was just looking for a local spot to work. Her teeth are perfect. Too perfect for this neighborhood. Her smile has captured my full gaze, and I look away in time to catch Bree looking through the small window of my office door.

"I'm gonna be honest with you, Sara," I interrupt her. "This shop is in the middle of what some would call the 'hood'. It's a dangerous place," I warn her.

"Is it?" she asks sarcastically. "Because I live just around the corner on Vernon Avenue."

"Yes, it is," I assure her. "Listen. I don't know why you moved to Brooklyn, but it's a rough place. And I know you probably think the cool thing to do is to live here but it's dangerous."

"I'm aware that Brooklyn is dangerous," she says softly. "But there are more dangerous places in the world than just Brooklyn. And I'm here for a job interview, not a neighborhood tour, with all due respect."

I'm shocked now. This lady is sharp. And attractive. But a Zombie, without a doubt.

"Besides," she continues. "If Brooklyn is so bad, why do you own a shop here?"

"Because," I tell her proudly, "I was raised here. And I love it. And I wanna show the people here that nice things and nice people still exist in this neighborhood. It's more than just the shoot-outs and gang violence they show on t.v."

"Interesting," she responds. "Where are you from?"

"I told you. I'm from Brooklyn."

"No, I mean where are you from?" She was serious now. "Do you know where your parents are from? And their parents before that?"

What the hell was this, a history lesson?

"I don't know," I say. "Why do you ask?"

"Well, you seem very overprotective about a place that is not even your home. I could understand if your ancestors were from here, but you seem to fight really hard for a place that you seem to have just wound up. Brooklyn isn't yours. You just exist here."

"Are you kidding me? This is my home. I've never been anywhere else. I was born here, will probably meet my wife here, raise my kids here and then die here."

"Right here in this coffee shop?" she joked.

"If I have to," I shoot back. I already know the type of girl that this chick is. She's that overly confident White girl that gets her kicks out of knowing more than everyone else about everything there is to know about anything. She's the type that goes around trying to educate other people on their 'roots' and trying extra

71

hard to be deep for no reason. I knew it from the moment she walked in that door a few minutes ago that she was no different than her grandfather's grandfather who probably rode into a town much like this one, tryna 'educate' niggas. And I get why it works—why her kind is called the 'Black man's kryptonite'. She's beautiful beyond my offense to her sharp personality.

"Okay, let's bring it back to the job interview," I tell her. "What are your thoughts about coffee?"

"I like it. The smell is nostalgic for me. I don't know how successful a coffee shop in this neighborhood could be, but it's better than another check cashing place or liquor store."

"What's that supposed to mean?" I ask.

"Well, coffee is good, don't get me wrong but you seem to be a pretty solid person. Why not create a space where other young guys could come and learn some things from you? Maybe even come and be recreational. Blow off some steam? The young people in this neighborhood seem to be angry about a lot of things. I wonder what it would be like if this place were just... different."

72

"So you're here on a job interview for a coffee shop, and you're trying to convince the owner that it shouldn't be a coffee shop?" I ask.

"Hey, I was just making a suggestion," she responds.

"If you must know," I tell her, "the previous owner of this building always complained about there not being good coffee in Brooklyn. So when she lost this place, I bought it before anyone else could. Then I turned it into a coffee shop. It used to be this candy shop where me and my boys would come to play video games and buy more junk food than we needed. This place raised us. When Pokémon was hot, it's where we all came to get cards. When Spice Girl lollipops dropped, Katy's candy had all the flavors with all the stickers. You know where I was when I found out that Skittles came out with SOUR SKITTLES?"

"Katy's?" she asks.

"No. I was in 297 park[11], but I ran to Katy's dammit," I joke again.

---

[11] Elementary school park where Lenny also had his first kiss. Although he and Bree went to P.S. 23, P.S. 297 had a better jungle gym.

"Hmm," she ponders.

"What are you thinking?"

"Well, if Katy's was such a great place for you and all your friends, why didn't you just pay for her to keep the place?"

"Or," she continued, "if you were gonna buy the place from her, why not just keep it a candy shop with games and all the popular candies you just told me about? Why not let it continue to be what it was for you and your friends growing up? Why try and reinvent the wheel? Why coffee?"

Before I can develop an answer, my phone vibrates in my pocket. It's Bree.

Baby Bro: You can't hire a Zombie. -_-

                          Me: Can you chill? Nobody is
                              hiring a zombie.

Baby Bro: Okay, I'm just saying. Cuz me
and Alexis are listening at the door and I feel like
you 'bout to be a little bitch and hire this Zombie.

And if you do, it'd be a huge mistake. So, yeah…

> **Me:** If you and Alexis are at the
> door, who's watching the shop,
> idiot?

"Here's the thing Sara," I say, "I don't think you'd be a good fit for the shop. The pay isn't very much. I hardly take home enough for myself each month."

"Why is that?" she asks.

"Well," I tell her, "If you'll notice on the menu board, we only do suggested prices here. I want people in this neighborhood to know good coffee but not have to break the bank to do so."

"Interesting," she says. "That's not very smart."

"Well it's my way of helping the neighborhood," I tell her.

"I don't think you're helping the neighborhood by offering high-quality coffee for 'suggested prices'. I think you're cheating them out of an opportunity to support your business and keep it afloat."

"Well, maybe I don't want their support. Maybe I know what it's like to not be able to afford nice things and I'd rather them enjoy something good for cheap," I shoot back.

"Okay," she responds calmly. "And then maybe you can explain that to the neighborhood when your business tanks."

This girl's got some nerve.

"You know what? I don't think we'll be needing your help after all," I tell her firmly. "Thanks for stopping by, though."

"Sure," she says, still keeping her cool. "Thank you for your time."

She extends her hand for a shake. I come from around the desk and meet her hand with mine. As she made her way out, I shout to her, "Alexis can make you a drink on the way out if you want."

"Oh, is it on the house or should I leave a suggested amount?" she shouts back. As she closed the door to the shop, I went out to meet Bree and Alexis, who were conveniently pretending to be working.

"How did it go?" Bree asks.

"Like you don't already know," I tell him. "She definitely wasn't a good fit."

"Good," he tells me. "Cuz for a second I thought you were into that chick."

4. "Ex-Factor" (Ms. Lauryn Hill)

When the day was over, and we closed down the shop, I waited for the B54 bus with Alexis. I don't really like him waiting by himself in this neighborhood or riding his bike home so late.

"You should come over for dinner, yo. I think Mami would be happy to see you."

"Nah," I tell him, "Lisaura would be pissed if I just showed up like that."

The truth is, I would love to go over to his house tonight. I honestly would use any excuse in the world to see Lisaura right now. I answered too quickly with that courtesy "no" and I kinda wish he'd ask again.

The bus pulls up, and from what I can see, it looks like a bunch of young dudes have taken up space in the back of the bus. I can tell these guys are up to no good because they're standing on the seats and laughing about something.

Dressed in red.

Fuckin' Bloods.

Probably from Roosevelt Projects. I know I'll have to get on and ride Alexis home now.

"I'm just gonna take you home, bro."

"You sure?" he asks. He can tell what I'm actually suggesting. It's too late to wait for another bus, and if I leave him alone, these niggas will definitely press him.

"Yeah, I'm sure. Grab your MetroCard," I tell him. We board the bus and intentionally sit in the front, away from the seven or eight dudes near the back of the bus. The bus driver pulls off and makes his way up Myrtle

Avenue, skipping stops whenever he notices no passengers are waiting on certain blocks. We almost make it to Ridgewood before the dudes in the back begin to make their way to the front of the bus. At first, I figure they're just getting off, but they passed the back exit to get to the front. I already know what's up. They're about to start trouble. One of them, reeking of alcohol, walks up to us and asks, "What's poppin'?"[12]

"Nothin' much," I tell them.

"Oh, aight," one of them says. I assume him to be the leader because the rest of 'em just line up behind him, looking like they're ready to follow his orders, if necessary.

"That's a nice bike," the main guy continues. This time he's looking at Alexis and Alexis grips the seat and handlebar to his bike like they had become extensions of his own body.

"What's that, a BMX?" the guy asks. I look at Alexis, giving him a face that says, "don't say anything."

---

[12] *"what's poppin'"* is often an innocent term used by friends that simply means, "what's up" or "what's going on?" In more serious instances, it is the way a member of the Bloods gang asks another person about their gang affiliation.

"Y'all niggas ain't gotta be scared. Ain't nobody tryna take your bike," one of them falsely assures us.

"We ain't scared of y'all," Alexis spits out.

Fucking idiot…

"Oh, no?" the guy asks, almost rhetorically. "We wasn't gon' fuck wit' y'all niggas but since y'all ain't scared, what's good? Get off the bus and let's get it poppin'"

"We good. It's not even that serious," I tell them.

"Nah, y'all niggas got heart, shoot the fair with me or one of my mans," he suggests. Just then the bus driver interrupts,

"Alright, that's enough."

He's an older guy. Old enough to be a grandfather to each one of us.

"Ain't gon' be no fightin' tonight. Y'all get off this bus and leave these boys alone."

"Fuck you, mista'," one of them screams back.

"Mind your language young man," the driver demands. "I'm sure those officers outside wouldn't appreciate you cursing at me like that."

We all look out the bus window and see four officers standing by a squad car near the bus stop. I'd never been happier to see a cop.

"Yeah, aight," the main guy says. "Y'all little niggas lucky," he continues as he and his boys exit the bus.

I'll never understand the younger generation. With everything going on in the news, the best thing they can be doing is tryna start a fight on the bus? I push the tape that lines the bus windows, and we get off at the Myrtle and Knickerbocker stop.

"Thanks for that," Alexis says, breaking the silence as we walk to his house.

"It's nothin', bro," I tell him.

As we walk up to his house, his mom is bringing the trash out to the curb.

"Lenny!" she screams in excitement. "Why you take so long no coming here?"

Her English wasn't so great, but I already knew I wouldn't be able to leave now. Lisaura's mom loves me.

"You stay for dinner, Si?"

"Um, I don't know Mrs. Vargas," I tell her, hoping she'll persist.

"None sense, Lenny. You stay. Come inside," she tells us.

"Told you," Alexis boasts.

As we make our way into the house, I can already smell what Lisaura's mom had been cooking. Smelled like lasagna, baked chicken, rice, beans and I just know there's some potato salad in there too.

I take a seat in the living room where Lisaura's grandmother is sitting. She's a racist old lady who never says much, but when she does talk, I don't understand it anyway. Alexis always translated the things she would say and it was always something about Black people. She could always form just enough English to say,

"Oh but not you, Lenny. You're good. Not like other Black people."

Alexis and Lisaura would laugh, and their mom would explain that she's just old— not racist, and that she grew up in a different time than us. I kinda understand, but Bree was not feeling it when he first experienced it. He walked out, screaming, "That lady racist as shit, yo. We outta here!" He refuses to come back here with me.

"What are you doing here?!"

It's Lisaura, standing in the doorway of the living room.

"Um, I was just riding Alexis home, but your mom made me come in for food. You know how she is," I tell her.

"Bullshit, Lenny," she snaps back. "You're just looking for an excuse to be here. I told you, we're done."

She was right. Part of me was concerned about Alexis' safety, but another part of me was also hoping I'd get invited in. And I'm glad I'm here. I almost forgot how beautiful Lisaura was. Standing there being all angry but sexy as hell.

"Can we just talk about this upstairs maybe? I don't wanna argue in front of your moms. Are the kids here?" I ask her.

"No," she says with almost no emotion in her voice. "They're with their dad this weekend."

"You talkin' to that nigga again?" I ask sternly.

"Wouldn't you like to know," she answers as she turned toward the steps. I knew she was just messing with me. Lisaura's a good girl. Spiteful, but a good girl. And I let her have that one just now because I really wanna make up with her this time. Whatever it takes.

We make our way up the stairs and into her bedroom.

Smells so good in here.

She shuts the door behind her and sits on the bed.

"What do you want, Lenny?"

What would Biggie think?

Ask for 'one more chance.'[13]

"I just want us to be back to normal," I say.

"Have you spoken to your brother about what he did?"

---

[13] *"One More Chance" - 1994*

"I have," I tell her. The truth is that I hadn't, but I knew she wouldn't wanna hear much more if I hadn't lied just now.

"And is he planning to apologize?" she asks.

"Why do you need an apology? Why can't we just move on?"

"Because, Lenny!"

"That's not an answer," I tease.

"You're so full of shit, Lenny. How come you don't never check your brother when he steps out of line? You let him get away with everything. He's rude, he's disrespectful, and nobody likes him. No one. You're the only person that likes him."

"I also like you," I tease again.

"No, Lenny. I'm not kidding. Not this time. Your brother disrespected me for all the world to see. And what did you do? You deleted the comment as if it never happened. I bet you never even spoke to him about it."

"You're right," I tell her. "I haven't spoken to him about it. But I'm just waiting for the right time to bring it up."

"You're not doing him any favors, Lenny. You have to check him when he's wrong. He's never gonna learn. He has no respect, Lenny. Especially when it comes to women. It's prolly cuz y'all never had a mother, but that's no excuse."

Silence.

I think she can tell she's offended me but I don't speak up to break the awkwardness now. I want her to feel it. It's my payback.

"I'm sorry," she says. "I didn't mean to say it like that."

"Nah, you're good. I get it."

Suddenly, I don't wanna make up anymore. I just wanna be home. Not feeling upset the way I do. First that woman in the shop earlier today and now Lisaura. I'm really winning with the ladies today.

"I think I'm gonna go," I tell her.

"Lenny, don't go. I'm sorry. I just wanted you to understand how hurt I was by what your brother did. I really have missed you. You know that, right?"

She reaches for my hand and pulls me closer to her. Looking down at her sitting on her bed makes me want to just crawl into her and sleep the way I do so well. It had been so long since her legs closed around my back and my head rested in her breasts. She stands up and pulls me in for a hug. It felt good to be holding her again. How is it that it only takes a moment for normal to rush back in? Too fast to get away from. Too strong to try and fight. You just gotta embrace it and let it carry you away.

"Lisaura, Lenny, ven a comer!"

Lisaura pretended not to hear her mom just now so I pretend, too. Besides, it was too late now. We're already undressed. Already getting back to normal. Fingers tracing each other's outlines and reacquainting our lips, in case they had become unfamiliar with how well they fit one another. Lisaura's mom calling us for food isn't the only distraction. Somewhere, one of our phones is vibrating like crazy. Could be my dad. Could be Justine.

Could be Bree.

"I'm just gonna get it," I tell her.

"Really?" she asks.

"It could be my dad," I tell her.

"Whatever."

It's Bree. But I'm not gonna answer it. Not this time. I'm gonna show Lisaura that I can put her before Bree. I turn my phone off and jump back into the bed. Our bodies reconnect like there was no interruption at all. And in between our kisses, I can feel Lisaura's smile go big, thanking me for the sacrifice I just made.

△ ▼ △ ▼

It's 2 am, and there's no use in going home now. Lisaura's already knocked out, and my mouth has dried in the way that sleep begins to invite itself. I wrap myself around her like she would float off of the bed if I let go. I also realize that for the second night in a row, I've forgotten to take my pill. No use in stressing about it now. Plus, I'm allowed to miss a few days.

Morning arrives, and I'm in no rush to be away from Lisaura. I couldn't care less about opening the shop on time, and I'm dreading the thought of turning my phone on again.

But I do.

Eighteen missed calls.

All Bree.

Five missed text messages.

All Justine.

I read them.

And now I'm crying, even though I don't want to be crying.

Justine: Lenny where tf are you??

Justine: Lenny, pick up your fucking phone!!!

Justine: Shit, Lenny you need to call your dad, ASAP!

Justine: Lenny, it's about your brother.

Lisaura wakes up, and she wants to know what's wrong, but I can't seem to make words come out. She's asking me if I'm okay, but I can't answer. All that I can hear is Justine's last text message in a voice that was probably panicking at the time.

Justine: Lenny, meet us at Woodhull Hospital.

Bree's been shot.

5. "Who Shot Ya?" (The Notorious B.I.G.)

Please don't be dead!

Please don't be dead!

Fuck, fuck, fuck!

How the fuck did Bree get shot?

Where was he at?

Who was he with?

Why the fuck did I turn my phone off?

Fucking Lisaura, shut up!

"Lenny, what is wrong, where are you going?"

"I gotta go to Woodhull," I finally say. "Bree's been shot."

"What?! How?" she asks.

"How the fuck am I supposed to know, Lisaura?!"

I went too far.

"I'm sorry. I didn't mean to yell. It's just that I was here with you all night and I don't know what happened. I just gotta go."

"I'm going with you," she decides aloud.

"No! I got it. Just... I got it. I'll call you," I assure her.

I rush out of Lisaura's house and run down Myrtle Avenue. Her house is just a few train stops from Flushing Avenue, where Woodhull hospital is but I can't seem to think straight. Somehow, the thought of my feet moving quicker than waiting for a train makes complete sense. At first, I run but running only makes me feel like I have to pee and shit at the same time. I stop on a corner and take a piss behind a giant Waste Management container. I completely disregard that it's

7 am, and Brooklyn is buzzing with buses and families rushing to church.

I zip up and reach for my phone. Justine isn't picking up her phone, and neither is my dad. Why didn't I just answer the phone last night? I make a right, down Broadway Avenue and I notice that about three M trains have passed over my head. I should've just waited for the train.

By the time I reach Woodhull hospital, I can't breathe and nearly collapse in the lobby. The hospital is quiet, and no one seems frantic. In fact, I appear to be the only person in a panic. It's obvious I'm the only person here with a brother that has a bullet in him.

"Hi, my name is Leonard Mitchell, my brother Brian Mitchell was admitted sometime this morning for a gunshot wound."

The woman at the front desk looks at me like I'm stupid.

"Slow down sir. What did you say your name was?"

"Leonard Mitchell," I tell her.

"And you're here to see who?" she asks.

"My brother, Brian Mitchell. B-R-I-A-N, Mitchell, M-I-T-C-H-E-L-L," I tell her in an annoyed tone. This is nothing like the movies. This woman is moving way too slow.

"Okay, your brother is in surgery on the third floor. I can give you a pass to wait there for him. There are already two people here to- ..."

"Can I just get a fucking pass? Please?!"

There's silence now as if everyone in the lobby had stopped to hear.

She looks at me and continues in an unbothered tone, "There are already two people here to see Mr. Mitchell so you can wait in the hall with them until the surgery is over. Here is your pass."

I snatch the pass from the woman and jog over to the elevators. Once I'm on, the doors close slower than I would like them to, but I'm still holding the button marked 'door closed'. There's a woman on the elevator with balloons and a teddy bear. Maybe she knows someone who gave birth. Maybe it's true that whenever someone dies, new life comes to take the place of the person who lost theirs. I can't remember when I last spoke to God, but I throw a quick prayer up anyway.

The doors open and I see my dad and Justine right away. They're sitting on a bench by a window at the end of the hall. Justine gets up and runs to me, her long braids flopping behind her. She would have fallen to the floor completely if I didn't think to put my arms out to catch her. She buries her face into my armpit and sobs deeply.

"Justine," I say with a stern voice. "Justine, it's gonna be okay. What are they saying about Bree?"

She pulls her face away from my torso and looks at me. Her eyes are puffy, and her face is dry.

"Where were you Lenny?" she asks in a disappointed tone.

"I was… I was busy. What happened, Justine? Who shot Bree?"

"I don't know," she says as she begins to cry again.

Suddenly, all I can think about is Bree's favorite movie. All I can see is his stupid smile that's too big for his face, and I start to cry too. I get it. The details aren't important right now. Sometimes you just have to stop and cry. I pull Justine back into me and hug her tightly.

Three hours later, the doctor comes out and asks to speak to my dad. This part actually does feel like the movies. My dad seems to be nodding his head in the 'yes' motion to whatever the doctor is saying. I didn't notice how much blood was on my dad's pants and work boots.

Shit.

Bree's really been shot.

My dad begins to cry now, which is weird because I've only seen my dad cry one time in my entire life. It was in 1997, and he was telling us the story about how Bree and I had a sister. She died as soon as she was born due to a hole in her heart. Me and Bree would've had an older sister. My dad said they didn't even have time to name her. He only cried for a little before he decided he didn't wanna be telling us that story anymore.

Me and Justine run over, expecting the worst. The doctor says he'll give us a moment and walks away.

"What did he say, pop?" I ask.

"The doctor says they removed eight bullets from Bree's body. Two of them from his right leg, and six from his torso. Two more are lodged behind his left shoulder, but they can't seem to remove them."

"But he's okay?" Justine interrupts.

"He's gonna be okay, but the doctor says it'll be a tough recovery."

"Thank God," I yell as my head falls back and my eyes find the back of my eyelids with relief. It feels like the first time I've blinked since I woke up at Lisaura's this morning.

"They're gonna move him into recovery, and we can come back and see him later tonight. For now, we should go home and get some rest," my dad insists.

"Nah, I'm staying," I protest.

"Me too!" Justine chimes in.

"Nonsense," my dad says firmly. "We'll go home, get cleaned up, and put some food in our stomachs. We'll come back first thing after dinner."

Injured Bree or not, both Justine and I know well enough not to contest my dad about something he's made his mind up about. So we head downstairs and return the visitors' passes to the front desk. Justine's car is illegally parked in front of the hospital, but even the cops around here know better than to ticket or tow her BMW. Justine's dad is the man in this city and is pretty well respected by the cops in this neighborhood.

I reach for the door handle of the back seat, but Justine won't unlock the door. I turn around, and both she and my dad are looking at me with faces sadder than the ones I found them with a few hours ago.

"What's up? Open the door, Justine," I tell her.

"Maybe you should sit up front, Len."

"Nah, I'll ride in the back. Let pops ride shotgun," I tell her.

"No son," my dad interrupts. "You sit up front."

"Why? I'm good if-" and then I finally get it. I look through Justine's un-tinted windows, and I can see why they want me to ride in the front so badly. The back seat is covered in blood. A thick, dark-red coat of half-dried blood is painted unevenly across Justine's beige, leather seats.

They drove Bree here.

99

They rushed my brother here in the backseat as he bled out from ten gunshot wounds.

"Who shot Bree, Justine?" I ask.

"Let's just go home," my dad interjects.

"Justine!" I shout. She looks at me and cries again this time.

"Who shot my brother?" I ask again.

"We don't know," she says.

The car ride home is silent but my mind is rushing with thoughts in the front seat. I begin making deals as I reason with my own thoughts:

> **"Okay, if I see three red cars before the next light then Bree won't die."**

We make a left onto Tompkins avenue, but I don't see the three red cars that were a part of the deal I made with myself a few seconds ago. I decide that the last deal doesn't count and it should have been blue cars instead.

"Guys, how do you not know who shot Bree but this car is drenched in his blood?" I ask.

Justine looks in the rearview mirror at my dad, almost as if she needed his permission to tell me what I wanted to know. My dad must've given her the look of approval because Justine starts to speak. She nervously grabs the wheel by both hands as if I were a road test instructor and then begins recounting what happened.

"Well, I got a call from Bree saying he was locked out of the house and that you weren't picking up your phone. He didn't wanna wake your dad, and he was too tired to go anywhere else," Justine explains.

"Why didn't he have his keys?" I ask. It only took two seconds before I realized how stupid and irrelevant that question was in the moment.

"He didn't say," she explains. "He just said that he really needed to get in the house and that he was locked out."

"Well, how did you get to him? Did you see him get shot?"

"That's the thing. By the time I got to your block, there were already people running and calling for the ambulance. I couldn't believe it, but when I looked, it was Bree. Bree was on the ground crying and bleeding a lot. A whole lot. I went and sat on the ground with him, but everyone else just ran. Your dad showed up and helped me get him into the car. We must've waited for twenty minutes, but there were no paramedics, so we just put him in the car. We rushed him here, and they took him away. We didn't even get a chance to explain what happened. They saw all the blood and your dad carrying Bree, and they just took him away on a stretcher."

"Okay, but was there anyone on the block? Did anyone see who shot him?"

"Yes," she says nervously.

My dad sat up and cleared his throat behind us. We pull up to the corner of Myrtle and Tompkins but can only make it as far as Mike's Pizzeria before we are forced to make a right turn. We can't get onto our own block. The street is blocked off with yellow police tape, and there are news vans everywhere.

"So if you saw the shooter, why didn't the guy run? Were the cops there? Did they arrest him?" I ask.

"That's the other thing, Lenny," my dad interrupted.   "The guy didn't run."

"Well, who was the shooter?"

"It was a cop," Justine says.

"A cop?" I ask as if I had heard wrong.

"Yeah a cop," my dad assures me. Justine begins crying again, but I refuse to join her this time. My dad put his hand on my shoulder as Justine pulled into a parking spot. My dad clears his throat again.

"The cop was Officer James," he says. "Officer James shot your brother."

6. "Fuck the Police" (N.W.A)

"Are you okay?" one of them asks. I can't really tell who.

"Yeah," I say.

And I wasn't lying. I'm really okay. Because I know that there's been a mistake. Officer James would not have shot Bree. There is just no universe where that's even remotely possible. We grew up playing hide

104

and seek with Officer James' kids. Granted, he once caught Bree kissing his daughter behind the handball court in Bartlett Park, but Bree was like twelve, and back then, he could be caught kissing just about anyone's daughter, and that's hardly a reason to shoot someone. No way. There's just no way. And since I've decided in my mind that there was no way, my dad and Justine need to hear it too.

"There's been a mistake," I say.

"What do you mean?" Justine asks. "Len, I saw it with my own eyes."

"You saw Officer James shoot Bree?" I asked sternly. I feel like she knew that I was asking her in a way that demanded she'd be sure.

"When I got there, Officer James was standing with his gun drawn and yelling into the radio on his shoulder. He was calling for backup or an EMT or something. I don't know."

"Well if you're not 100% sure then you can't say stuff like that," I tell her pretty roughly. "Also, how the hell did you get Bree into your car if an officer shot

Bree? Wouldn't they have blocked off the scene and stopped people from getting close?"

"I guess so," she said, "but when an ambulance didn't show up for a while, your dad pretty much threatened Officer James into letting us take Bree to the hospital before he died on the street or something."

"Okay, enough now," my dad interrupts. "Let's figure out how we're gonna get into the house and get cleaned up."

Just then, Justine's dad calls and tells her that we need to get over to their house, quickly. I can already guess what it's about to be like. Justine's dad works for the Brooklyn congressional district. I'm not sure what that means aside from the fact that he sits on a bunch of important boards and is always trying to get me and Bree to come out and encourage the community to vote. Justine's dad is always around for a photo-op, or to lead a peaceful protest and tell you why he needs your vote for some election that's happening. And if this call is anything like what I've seen of him in the past, I know two things for sure: we'd have a dope place to get cleaned up and Justine's dad is about to turn this into a political spin for himself.

"My dad says that your street has been shut down for investigative purposes. He said that we need to avoid the media and that you and your dad are welcome to get cleaned up at our place until this thing blows over."

Justine has a good point. If what they're telling me is true— if there's a chance that Officer James actually shot Bree, then this is about to turn into something huge.

"Okay," I say. "Let's go to your house."

Justine pulls out of the parking spot and pops the most illegal U-turn that I've ever seen in my life. She must be doing like forty-five on regular streets, but again, Justine's pretty much got a pass in this town. Her, her dad, and her step-mom live in this friggin' mansion up in Highland Park. Some say that Highland Park is considered Queens territory, others argue that it's Brooklyn. I just say it's rich as hell. At a glance, you'd think it's just some weird in-between place before you hit the Jackie Robinson Expressway, but it's a pretty wealthy neighborhood if you stop and look.

We pull up to Justine's house, and it's just as regal as it always looks. The grass is green, the trees around it are high, and none of the big ass windows have curtains on 'em. You could see straight into the place.

"Sweetheart," Justine's dad met us in the driveway. "Are you okay? How is Brian doing?"

"Let's talk about it inside," she insists.

"Of course, baby girl. Mr. Mitchell, Lenny," he says as he shakes both our hands. I could see why some people don't like this guy. He's just always on. Always being a politician.

"How's it going, Mr. Harris?" I ask rhetorically. Of course, he provided an answer.

"I'm fine, but I can't imagine how you two must be feeling. Please, come inside."

I hate how he's speaking. His voice is remorseful and overly comforting as if Bree is already dead or something. This house is too perfect. The couches we sit on are too expensive, and his wife is too nice, bringing us drinks even when we were sure in our answers about not wanting more than a shower and maybe some new clothes to change into. I don't wanna talk about how I feel, and I don't want any of this help if I'm being completely honest. I just want to be at the hospital with Bree. What happens if he wakes up and no one is there? But Justine's dad had a good point.

"Even if you guys could go home, the media and news outlets are probably camped out at your front door."

"They are," Justine assures him. "We drove by right before you called."

"Look, guys," Mr. Harris says firmly, "I have a lot of connections in Brooklyn. I can help you navigate this thing if you want. I've known your family for a long time, and it would be crazy for me not to offer my knowledge and resources. I see things like this happening to families all the time, and they make so many mistakes. They get in front of the news cameras and say the wrong things. They hire the wrong lawyers-"

"Lawyers?" my dad interrupts.

"Yes, lawyers." Mr. Harris reassures him. "But I want to help. And obviously at no cost to your or your family."

Justine can hardly hold back her smile. I can tell this means a lot to her. Heck, I wouldn't be surprised if she hadn't already spoken to her dad about all of this before we got here. Bree means a lot to her. I get that.

We all pick a bathroom and shower. Yeah, there are like five bathrooms in this place. Mr. Harris provides a change of clothes for me and my dad. Just some jeans, running shoes, and most conveniently, two of his recent campaign shirts. The shoes don't fit, but I don't complain. He has his driver take us back to the hospital and gives us two very explicit instructions:

Do NOT talk to news reporters or post anything to social media until he gets us a lawyer.

Do NOT Google the shooting.

I, of course, pull one of Bree's moves. I don't Google it. Heck, I don't even look at CNN or Brooklyn 12 to see if it's made headlines or anything. Instead, I pull up Twitter. Because Mr. Harris didn't say anything about looking at Twitter. While the driver is weaving through cars down Bushwick Avenue, I realize that I've always wondered what the inside of a Sprinter looked like. It's a bit anticlimactic.

I've also always wondered what it was like to see someone you know on social media being hashtagged. I didn't have to wonder for too long because it's exactly what happened today. As the driver passed Richie's Gym, which is about five minutes from the hospital, I sat in a tinted Sprinter reading tweets about Bree on my phone. People are already talking. People that I don't know.

#BrianMitchell

@queen_gotherown85- "Here we go again. Another one of our brothers shot down. #BLM"

@blickkybeenon- "Smh... Damn shame how they shot that kid in cold blood."

@JohnTaylor225522- "I support the Brooklyn law enforcement. We cannot make an excuse for the youth that terrorize our streets!!"

Who are these people? They don't know us. They don't know Bree. They weren't there! Bree is not a gang member or hoodlum. He's my brother. He wouldn't hurt a fly. He's not a thug or a troublemaker. And now I'm crying. Not aloud or noticeably. Tears are just falling from my eyes as if the inside of my head is flooding and there's nowhere else for them to go.

I know what I need to do. I've gotta call Officer James. He can straighten the whole thing out. He was there. I know he didn't shoot Bree, but I just need to hear him say it. I need him to tell me that the investigators will not find any of the shell casings from his gun on the sidewalk of our street. I know he didn't shoot Bree.

So I call him.

No answer.

I call again.

Still no answer. I'll leave a message this time. Besides, Mr. Harris only said that we should avoid the news and Google. Another page from Bree's book. Bree loved finding technicalities.

"Hey Officer James, it's Lenn-"

"Are you stupid?" Justine yells. I get the feeling she wasn't looking for me to answer. She snatches my phone and presses a button. She lifts the phone to her ear and then pulls it away to press another button. Then she throws my phone at me even though I didn't have my hands up to catch anything.

"Why'd you do that?" I ask.

"Officer James is one of the suspected shooters on your brother's case- and yes, it's a case at this point- and you think it's wise to be calling him right now? I deleted your dumb-ass message. You're welcome, idiot."

Justine was right. How could I have tried to call Officer James right now? He's probably at a precinct trying to get his story together. Or maybe he's at the hospital wanting to see Bree. I don't know what to think. I just can't believe that Officer James had anything to do with shooting Bree. Maybe he was there to help last night.

We pull up to the hospital, and there are news vans everywhere. It takes a while before we can actually get out of the car but when we do, there is a bunch of yelling. Cameras are being shoved into our faces, and reporters are screaming at us. In all of the chaos, I hear questions about Bree and questions about how the family is coping, all being shouted at us at once. My dad, Justine, and I push through the crowd and make it to the hospital lobby. One thing is for sure: this had absolutely become a thing. A huge thing.

The process to check in is different now. The hospital has to be sure that no one from the media gains access to Bree's room and so now, we're being escorted to his room. We've also been patted down and told that no one is allowed in Bree's room except for us. All of this felt too crazy to be true. Twenty-four hours ago, I was lying next to Lisaura.

Bree's nurse is nice. She makes sure we're comfortable and even offers to bring in an extra cot for my dad to lay down on. None of us had gotten any sleep, and I honestly didn't want to. I'm too afraid of what my dreams might be about. So I pull up a chair and just stare at Bree. He doesn't look very different. His eyelashes are still way too long and it just looks like he's in a good sleep. His lips are chapped, and his hair needs to be brushed. He'd be upset if anyone saw him like this.

"But it's okay. Bree's just asleep," I tell myself.

Bree is asleep, and there's nothing we can do to wake him up except wait. So my dad and Justine fall asleep on the chairs up against the wall. Everyone is asleep. And so I sleep too.

You know how you kinda dream about what you hear as you're asleep? Well, I had a dream that I was trying to disable this bomb that was attached to my coffee shop. I had scissors in my hand, and I couldn't figure out which wire to cut. Before I know it, the beeping from the bomb is louder and faster, and then I'm not even dreaming anymore. I'm awake, and now two nurses rush in and are pressing a bunch of buttons and trying to get the beeping to stop. Suddenly, I'm not allowed to lay next to Bree, and the nurses are asking us not to panic.

It turns out, Bree's body went into shock while we were all knocked out. The nurses figure out how to stabilize him within minutes, but Justine is still crying. The nurses assure us that what happened is normal and that Bree's body is just dealing with the trauma of being shot a bunch of times and then undergoing a three-hour surgery all in one day.

"There's nothing to worry about, guys," one of the nurses says. "I've seen this a bunch of times, and it looks like your brother is gonna recover just fine. You just gotta have faith."

Faith in what?

I look at my phone, and I've managed to sleep through twenty-seven missed calls and ninety-three text messages. I glance over the names, and they're mostly just people we know from the neighborhood. A few of the texts simply ask, "Are you guys okay??" or "Yo, what happened bro?!" Only one text stands out from them all. It's from Lisaura.

> **Lisaura**: Lenny, please call me when you can. I know me and your brother don't have the best relationship but no one deserves to die. Is it true what the news is saying? Did Bree try to pull out a gun on a cop?! That's crazy. I would have never thought. Anyway, I'm just super concerned. I love you, forever and always. Please text me or call me when you can. Alexis is worried too.

I know that Lisaura can't be blamed for what happened, but I'm just really pissed that I was with her

117

when all of this went down. If I weren't with her last night, Bree wouldn't be on this hospital bed with tubes in his nostrils. I try my best to construct a reply, but I don't really know what to say. I know that I love her. I know that I want Alexis to know that everything is gonna be okay. I know how much he looks up to Bree. I know I want to tell Lisaura that I agree, Bree would never hold a gun, let alone point one at a cop. But I just don't know how to put all the words together.

Justine's dad walks in and interrupts my thoughts. He's dressed like he's headed to a very important business meeting and I can't help but think that we're going to have to talk about lawyers and interviews again. I mean, I've seen the families of Eric Garner and Alton Sterling on t.v. and I wonder if that's what we were gonna have to do. What if Bree doesn't pull through? How could this be happening to us?

"Hey folks," Mr. Harris says eagerly. I don't know if this man is actually this annoying or if I'm just annoyed that he's the only person who seems to be doing okay with everything that's been going on.

"So I've spoken to a few lawyers, guys that I trust, and they say that depending on how the investigation unfolds, we may have a pretty good case against the city." For some reason, I trust Mr. Harris in this moment. Especially if he's willing to make a case against the city he works for.

"If it turns out that Brian was shot unjustly," he continues, "we could have a pretty serious lawsuit on our hands."

"What about Officer James?" my dad asks.

"Well, he and the police commissioner are holding a press conference so that a statement can be released."

"When?" I ask quickly.

"At 10 pm. In a few minutes, actually," he answers.

This is great. Officer James will be able to clear this whole thing up, and the whole world will see that this is just a big misunderstanding. Officer James did not shoot Bree and Bree didn't have a gun.

My dad asks for one of the nurses to have a t.v. turned on for us. She reluctantly informs us that

119

television service for the room will cost us nine dollars a day, almost as if we're unable to pay it. Mr. Harris hands her a credit card and asks her to, "please provide the family with whatever they need" and for her not to mention anything about costs again.

I appreciated that.

The t.v. service is turned on, and Justine turns it to channel twelve. We've missed about eight minutes of the press conference, but the police commissioner is speaking now. We're all about to find out what happened last night.

"You okay?" Justine asks me.

"I'm okay," I tell her.

Really I'm just nervous. We all pay attention to the t.v. and silently agree that no one should say a word right now. The police commissioner begins his address in a serious tone.

"This morning at approximately 2:15 am, a call came through to our dispatchers about a robbery on the corner of Tompkins and Vernon

Avenue. Our units responded to the call and at 2:21 am, Officer Kenneth James and his partner arrived at the scene and found a Mr. Brian Mitchell yielding a firearm."

"That's not true!" Justine yells. "Lenny, that's not true!"

"Let him finish, Justine," I tell her calmly. I don't care about what this guy says. It's his job to make his men look good. I'm waiting for Officer James to tell his side. That's all I care about. He won't lie. I just know it. The commissioner continues,

"Officer James instructed Mr. Mitchell to lower his weapon to the ground and to step away from it with his hands raised. After the assailant refused to comply, Officer James warned that he would open fire in order to subdue him. The assailant appeared to point his weapon in the direction of Officer James, and as a result, my men were left with no choice but to open fire on the assailant in order to protect themselves and the people in the surrounding area. Our condolences go out to this young man's family, as we hear he is in Woodhull hospital recovering from multiple gunshot wounds. While we are aware that these kinds of scenarios can unfold at any moment, it is never an officer's hope to have to fire his weapon while on duty. A full investigation is still underway and there will be more details to come as we learn more. As of right now, the situation is being looked at as a crime against an N.Y.P.D. officer, with Mr. Brian Mitchell as the aggressor in the situation. We are working very closely with city prosecutors as we prepare to make a case against Mr. Mitchell and the two people who removed his body from the crime scene. I'd now like to invite Officer

Kenneth James to the podium to share
his account of the events."

"That's bullshit!" Justine yells again. This time
she shouted through tears and I'm thinking that I'd
never seen Justine cry as much as I'd seen in the past
twelve hours. Not when her mom and dad got divorced.
Not when she too learned about Travis Simmons
molesting me in the seventh grade and not even when
B2K announced their breakup back in freshman year of
high school.

Officer James takes to the podium and he looks
different than normal. His back is slumped, and so he
doesn't look his true six feet and four inches tall. His
eyes are heavy as if he slept less than we did today.
His hair is disheveled, and his expression is unsure. It's
as if we aren't looking at Officer James at all. He opens
his mouth slowly and begins to speak.

"The commissioner has explained
exactly what happened in the early
hours of this morning. I responded
with my partner to the scene, where I

123

found Brian Mitchell holding a gun. After urging the young man to drop his weapon and surrender, we were left with no options other than to wound the assailant in order to subdue him. My partner and I feel that we acted in compliance with the training and practices of an N.Y.P.D. officer and it's unfortunate that the situation has resulted in this way. My condolences go out to the family and I hope that the young man pulls through. I know that footage from the dash-cam of my police cruiser will be released tomorrow but I am confident that it will show evidence that supports my account of what happened. That is all."

That was it. Officer James turned from the cameras and walked out of the press conference.

Justine is crying.

My dad is yelling.

Mr. Harris is trying to calm them and I cannot move in the midst of all of this.

It's true.

Officer James shot Bree, and now he's addressed the public about it. According to him, Bree did have a gun. Officer James spoke about Bree as if he didn't even know him. As if he didn't know us. I was just in my shop talking to him yesterday. I don't understand any of this.

If what I heard is correct, not only is Bree gonna have to fight for his life in this hospital, but he may be looking at criminal charges if he even makes it through. So would Justine and my dad for trying to help save Bree's life. How is that possible? How could they be looking at jail time?

"No," I say aloud. "This is just a misunderstanding. We need to wait to see that dash-cam footage."

"Are you serious?" Justine asks rhetorically. "Officer James is not the man you keep trying to make him out to be. He's gonna look out for himself and his partner in all of this."

"But he's not like them!" I say. "He's not like the rest of the police."

"Fuck the police," someone said in a weak, raspy attempt.

It was Bree.

7. "Lost One" (Jay Z featuring Chrisette Michele)

Bree had been awake for longer than we were aware. He explained that he didn't have enough energy to get our attention as we watched the press conference but when he could finally will his lungs to push enough air through to his vocal cords, only one phrase was worth the effort.

> Fuck.
> The po.
> lice.

"And fuck you too, Lenny," he said more powerfully this time, almost as if his energy had slowly begun returning to him.

"Woah, fuck me?" I ask.

"Watch your mouths!" my dad shouts.

But Bree just continued on as if he and I were the only people in the room.

"Yeah, fuck you, Lenny. Fuck you for not being there last night. Where were you? And fuck you for not being here right now."

"What are you talking about, I've been here since yesterday! We all have!"

"Nah, I'm talking about being here for me. You're so hung up on Officer James being 'Deputy Do-Right' that you can't even accept that he shot me."

"What are you even talking about? There's dash-cam footage that will be released tomorrow. We'll see the truth."

"What truth?!" Bree might be overexerting himself now. "What truth, Lenny? That I had a gun? That I pointed a gun at Officer James?"

"No," I tell him. "Proof that he may have— I mean, it sounds stupid out loud, but I just think there's something missing here."

"I'm lying in a hospital bed, Lenny. What more is there to know? You're waiting on some footage to prove I didn't deserve to be shot? That's bullshit."

"I'm just saying—"

"You're saying a bunch of nonsense, yo. But I'm not even surprised," Bree assures me. "This is what you do. You're always tryna be the fucking mayor to everybody. God-forbid someone doesn't like you, Lenny. Get off the fence and fucking be here for me, man. I can't believe I'm even having to tell you this."

"Bruh, I'm here. What else do you want?"

"You think I had a gun, Lenny?" He asks me this as if to start a brand new conversation. Like everything we said before didn't count, and this is a new point he's trying to make.

"I'm just saying there's two sides, but if you need me to say it, no, I don't think you had a gun, or would ever hold a gun. You happy?" I ask.

"That's what I'm talking about. You do and say shit to make people happy. Just say what you mean, man. You would take Officer James' side over your own brother's. That's just who you are. It's whatever man."

"It's who I am?" I ask. "I'm always on your side!"

"Then where were you when I was calling you? Tell me where you were when you got the news about me being here? About me being shot and having to fight for my life in this shitty hospital."

I couldn't tell Bree that I was at Lisaura's house when he needed me the most. It would be the cherry on top of this already messed up argument. The truth is that I had failed Bree. Not always but definitely this time. And what a time to get it wrong. I'm always there for Bree. He knows that. At least, I thought he knew.

"I was caught up with some stuff," I tell him.

"You were caught up with Lisaura," he retorts. And now it feels like whatever air was left in the room has suddenly been sucked out.

"Yeah," he continues. "The person who did respond last night was Alexis. He told me you took him home last night and I'm pretty sure that's where you were. I hope the sex was worth it. I'm here because of you. So why don't you go back to the people you really care about? Go be with your family, Lenny."

"You're buggin'," I tell him. "You're talking through anger, and I'm just gonna let you be mad for a while."

"Oh, I'm not mad," he assures me. "I'm good. It just is what it is. This is who you are. Go be a dad to Lisaura's kids. I'm not mad at you. I just know who you are now."

"Lemme get this right," I start. "You're upset because I wasn't near my phone?!"

"No," he yells this time, "I'm mad because I'm not safe with you."

"What are you even talking about?" I ask him. I genuinely ask him because I'm confused.

And so he responds with a question in true Brian fashion. "What is the one thing every woman would say she wants most from her man?"

"I don't know," I say, "attention?"

"No, Lenny. Security. Every woman wants security. And you let me down, yo. I don't feel safe with you."

"Bree, I'm not your fucking significant other. And I'm not your parent! I'm your brother! I'm hurt too. I deal with the same abandonment and fucked up social issues that you do, but I don't blame you for it."

"It's fine, Lenny. It is what it is," he assures me.

There's nothing I can really say. I've never seen Bree like this. I've never seen him this angry at me. I've never seen him okay without me. My dad and Justine are probably just as shocked as I am. Standing awkwardly by the door is Mr. Harris with a box of Dunkin Donuts that he never really got to offer everyone.

I failed to mention to you that I hate hospitals. Or maybe I did mention it. Idunno. Back when doing wrestling moves on your siblings was the thing to do, I once Rock-bottomed[14] Bree onto the couch, and he bounced into the coffee table. His head hit one of the corners, and he bled all over the wood floors in our

---

[14] Signature wrestling move by Dwayne "The Rock" Johnson.

132

living room. On the way to the emergency room, my dad kept going on and on about how I could've killed Bree and how I was gonna have to explain what I did in case a social worker might ask. Needless to say, Bree took his twelve stitches like a champ. The doctor said he was such a good kid and that Bree didn't flinch once. He sat up on the hospital bed fighting back tears and making sure we knew that he was okay. He wouldn't let us see him cry. He also wouldn't let me take the fall for him having to get stitches.

> **"Don't worry about it, Lenny. It was my fault. I was being too dramatic like the real-life wrestlers. I kinda threw myself into that table."**

He was lying back then. To protect me.
It was my fault.
But that was just like Bree to take the fall for people. His heart is too big. His shoulders are so broad. He's always protecting people from feeling embarrassed or at fault. But this was not the Bree

laying in front of me today. He had made it clear that I fucked up. Big time. So I do the only thing I can think of in this moment. I turn and leave. I leave because there's nothing left to say. I leave because I'm embarrassed. I leave because I thought I knew what it meant to be here for Bree and my dad but apparently, I don't. I wonder if my mom left because she didn't know how to be here either. I wonder what I will eat with my pill tonight or if I'll even have the appetite to eat at all. Which reminds me again that I didn't even take my pill last night.

Mr. Harris is behind me as I press for the elevator in the hall to get me outta here. I can't tell whether he cares or if he's concerned I'll speak to the media on the way out. Either way, I'm glad he's here. Makes me feel like less of a dick for walking out just now. I guess there's no right way to walk away from your best friend and your dad after your only brother admits that you suck as a human being. Bree and I have fought before but this time was more serious. I get the feeling that lately, I've been on the edge of losing the people closest to me. I'm almost certain I've just lost one.

We reach the lobby, and I can already see the reporters and news vans as I walk swiftly toward the doors. It's dark out, but these guys never leave. They just camp out, waiting for a story. As I get closer, I can't help but think that this part doesn't feel like the movies either. The people with microphones must recognize who I am because there is a complete gearing-up that begins to happen. Hand motions are waved in the air which I assume translates to, "Get the cameras rolling, it's about to go down!"

Before I push on the revolving door to leave the hospital, Mr. Harris grabs the back of my shirt and gives me a stern look. I'm not sure if the look is permission for what he knows I am about to do or if it is a look that is warning me of how I'm about to act stupidly. I think he and I at least agree that silence is no longer an option.

The roundabout through the revolving door seems like an eternity, a silence I've never experienced as I can barely hear muffled yelling and cameras snapping. Quick glimpses of the News 12 logo and red lipstick on one of the reporters are all I can make out in all of the chaos. And then I emerge from the silence as the noise slowly seeps into the small space I'm pushing through. Without hesitating, I answer the first question I can hear clearly.

"Mr. Mitchell, how is your brother holding up?!"

They know my name.
What would Biggie do?

'Never let them know your next move. Don't you know Bad Boys move in silence and violence?'[15]

Fuck it.

---

[15] *"Ten Crack Commandments" - 1997*

"My brother is not okay," I say. I can't see much of anything, but that doesn't stop me from saying too much about everything.

"My brother is not okay, and neither am I. My family is not okay. We're hurt and upset. The world knew nothing about my brother up until about a day ago, and even now your understanding of him is jarred. You believe whatever the news outlets have told you, whether it be the local news or whichever website that a Google search led you to. Good or bad, the truth is that no one can decide who he really is. None of you know him. And if he is guilty of what the police have charged him with, then I don't really know him either. But if there is anyone who could be trusted to give an accurate account that would be closest to the truth, if there is anyone who could best determine who that man lying in a hospital bed up there is, my guess is that it would be me. So what I'll tell you is what I've seen of him. My brother is kind and big-hearted. In 2003, I watched Bree walk old ladies up and down flights of stairs with a flashlight because there was a blackout for two days and no one did anything to stop people from being robbed in the dark staircases of the housing projects. In 2008, he sold his sneaker collection and gave all the money to Our Lady of Sorrows when he heard they were closing it down because the church wasn't doing well. Those things don't matter though because you all have made up your minds. You've already decided that nothing good, or even decent could come from where we live. This place wasn't even deemed livable until about ten years ago. Suddenly, the ghetto is being sought after. Tell me, when will we be enough? You put a cap on what we're allowed to be and where we're allowed to be and then crucify us for using the only things you've allowed us."

Suddenly, this isn't about Bree anymore, and while I'm fully aware of this, I can't bring myself to stop talking. Mr. Harris is holding a firm tug at my shirt again. I take a second to look back at him, and now his look is different. Again, I can make only two guesses about what his look means. It's either saying, "You're going too far," or "Keep going, son." Either way, his grip on my shirt says one clear thing: I'm with you.

So I continue.

"You tell our women that the standard for beauty is something that their bodies and hair simply cannot ever be and they're left to hate themselves for it. What's more, is you mock them in their attempts to reach the impossible goal that you set for them. When the picture of success is a white picket fence in suburbia, a perfect credit score, 2.5 kids, a few degrees, and a 401k, everyone on this side of White is immediately disqualified. I can't speak for the Latino or for the Asian. But I can speak for my people. My hurting, frustrated, misunderstood Black people, who are one of the most type-casted, exploited, and dehumanized groups of people on the planet, WHILE SIMULTANEOUSLY are the most emulated, as well. How can that be? How do you glorify the art and massacre the artist? Why is 'White' the standard?" I ask with almost no transition or even a concern for there needing to be one. "If being White, whether in skin tone or in the ideological sense of the word, is what we've deemed the standard, then many of us have lost the race before the starting shot has even been fired. Who even are you people with your microphones and cameras? Where do you sleep at night and what roads do you take to come here whenever there is a story to put on display for the world? How have we become your favorite reality show? In the place we were given to live, using resources we've been allowed, we have become your favorite thing to watch. The saddest part is that I never understood how daunting it all really is until me and my family went from being extras to the main attraction, all in one night. And so here's a little behind scenes scoop from one of the main characters. I can tell you about my co-star. I can tell you who he is not. He is not the person that the news and the police commissioner have made him out to be. He's never owned or even held a gun. He wouldn't. He couldn't."

I don't know when the flashing sounds on the cameras stopped. Perhaps it was when I started talking about White being the standard, I don't know. But the front of Woodhull hospital is quiet now, and people have stopped to watch. Above us, there are onlookers watching from the platform at the Flushing train stop. The reporters have all lost the enthusiasm in their faces, and I'm not sure what to do now. One reporter in the back of the crowd is near the street. He stands on his tippy-toes and makes himself seen in order to ask one question:

"Who are you talking to?"

"What do you mean?" I ask him. Everyone turns his way and makes room for him to be seen now. He's a short man, maybe Justine's height. His hair was disheveled and his notepad a mess. Realizing that we're all waiting for him to clarify his question, he stands up straighter and projects his voice over the sounds of the camera flashes starting up again.

"Well," he starts. "You said a bunch of stuff just now, and I don't know about anyone else here, but I can't seem to be able to tell who you're addressing. So my question is, who are you talking to? Who is that message to?"

I don't think about an answer because the truth is that the message was more of a rant.

To anyone.

To everyone.

And now I know what I want to say.

"The message is for whomever," I shout to him. "To whom it may concern," I say sarcastically, accompanied by air quotes.

Mr. Harris puts his arm around me and escorts me through the now vacant but shrinking space the crowd has made. Lucky for us, Mr. Harris' driver never left the spot he dropped us off at. We jump in, and the driver peels off, needing no instruction or direction. Mr. Harris is whispering something to the driver, but I can't make out what he's saying.

And then it hits me.

What did I just do?

What did I just say?

Who might I have offended?

Did I just make things worse for Bree's case?

I am so stupid.

Where is my phone?

My phone is in my pocket, where it's supposed to be but I don't feel I am where I should be. And I'm not just talking about this van, I'm talking about in time and space. All I want to do is get out of here. Right now, this van is all that is real, and I wish it would just disappear. Times like these make me close my eyes and retreat to a year that wasn't as stressful. Any year but this one, really. I think I'll go back to 2003. Kanye West just dropped "Slow Jamz", and I'm running around my high school gym trying my best to rap Twista's part of the song. I'll ride the G train home with my friends, and we'll do our handshake at every train stop that requires one of us to get off. I'll get home, and Maroon 5 will be on the t.v. singing about a girl who will be loved. Bree will have picked my bedroom lock and is laying on my bed with his filthy sneakers on.

Yeah, that's it.

It's 2003.

8. Interlude I (Lenny feat. Bree)

"Yo, Len."

"What?"

"You sleep?"

"Obviously not. And it's
'are you <u>asleep</u>?' you idiot."

"Whatever, nigga. Listen… What do you think about that story, we heard in Sunday school today?"

"Which one, Bree?"

"The one about those twin brothers, Jacob and Esau."

"What about it? And stop pushing your feet into my mattress before I come down there and punch you."

"My bad. But um… I can't stop thinking about what the Bible said. You know, about how God loved Jacob but he hated Esau. I mean, they weren't even born yet."

"Yeah, so?"

"Idunno. That's pretty fucked up."

"Go to sleep, Bree."

9. Dear No One (Tori Kelly)

"Wake up, kid. You're viral!"

It was Mr. Harris. He had meant 'viral', as in something was buzzing on social media, not 'viral', as in my health condition.

"Have you looked on Twitter?" he asks, which is pretty annoying seeing as how he's the one who woke me up just now. I guess I should consider that the question didn't need an answer. I open my phone and ignore the millions of unread text messages flooding my inbox.

"Search #TWIMC," Mr. Harris tells me.

And then I see it. I started something. Something was definitely going on. The tweets read as follows:

#TWIMC I don't hate u, I hate ur privilege
#TWIMC I've tried but my hair won't go flat and my curves won't go straight. #sorrynotsorry
#TWIMC What shall we do now that your grandfathers have brought us here but now y'all don't want us?
#TWIMC Don't tell me that we're crazy when America's genocide is called 'Thanksgiving'. Don't tell me this ain't happened b4. Don't tell me it can't happen again.
#TWIMC I'm just here to listen.

#TWIMC We're America's foster kids. We don't know our biological origins. We're stuck in this permanent trauma.

#TWIMC get over it. Slavery is over!

#TWIMC it's hard to say what you owe us. How do you put a price on art, music, food, ideas, culture, and thoughts? Perhaps we should consult the Native Americans. What did they charge you?

#TWIMC Germans were taught to hate the Jews so that their murders seemed justified. How should black America prepare for its genocide?

#TWIMC 'I love u' is all I want to say but I'm afraid of adding to what is already so loud.

#TWIMC You whisper the word black as if it's profanity.

#TWIMC Cite your sources and stop plagiarizing our shit!

I close my phone. What did I do? #TWIMC literally stands for 'to whom it may concern'. I started a movement. People were expressing themselves with no specific recipient in mind. They may as well have started those tweets with, "Dear No One".

Shit.

This is what Mr. Harris meant.

I had gone viral.

A few years ago, the word viral meant something completely different to me. The first time I heard it was at a clinic in Elmhurst, Queens two seconds after realizing that

my worst nightmare had come true.

"We'll try it one more time to see if it's gonna be."

"If what's gonna be?" I asked her.

"It's fine, don't worry. There's nothing to worry about," She assured me. "The mouth swab can usually tell but I'm gonna prick your finger and this time we'll see if it's gonna be."

"Well, does this usually happen? I mean, I'm not gonna become violent or anything but can I just see the first test?"

I don't know who trained this Indian woman on how to administer an HIV test but I'd sure like to meet the person. I have a few words for whoever deemed her fit to do her job. She hardly spoke any English, and I'm no racist, but if your job involves telling people whether or not they have a life-threatening disease, you'd better have more to say than "We'll see if it's gonna be."

I can admit that I was a bit on edge but if there was any way to find out that you're HIV-positive, it sure as hell would suck to have found out by way of the lady who wasn't sure how to tell if it was 'gonna be'.

'Gonna be' what?

I'd been in these offices before. I know how it goes. You take a number. You fill out a form. They call your number. They ask you a bunch of questions.

When was your last HIV test?
What were the results?

Why do you feel you need an HIV test
today?
Did you have unprotected sex with
someone you think has HIV?
Are you in a relationship?
Do you have sex with women or men?
Both?
So you're bisexual?
Oh, you're just with women now?
But you've been with men in the past?
So you're bisexual...

Whatever. This wasn't supposed to be any different. What did she mean she needed to do the test again? Was the first one positive? Is it wrong?

"Can I go to the restroom?" I asked.

"Yes, but you can't leave."

"I won't, I just need to use the restroom," I assured her. I needed to pray. But I also had to poop, so I wasn't lying.

"God, please. Please, please, please, please. I'll stay off of Craigslist and out of the booths just please don't let me have HIV? Please??"

The truth is, I'd played this game for too long. Visiting the video booths just because I missed the smell of poppers and musk. Snooping through Craigslist to see if much had changed. None of that mattered now. Or maybe it mattered completely. Either way, my stomach was trying its hardest to exit my body through my butt. I prayed, pooped, and then walked back to that tiny room where the Indian lady was checking the timer next to my new test.

The timer had gone off. She still couldn't determine the results. So she called her superior into the room even though I had already seen both the tests by now. This was not like the other visits when I was told that I was fine and then warned about the importance of safe sex. The mouth swab and finger prick both showed the same result. Two pink lines, clear as day. Well, one sharp red line. The line below the red one was faint and pink. But if we're calling a spade a spade then I was spade positive. Who knows how long I'd been positive at that point. I was twenty-three years old and in a great heterosexual relationship with a Christian girl. How the fuck could I be HIV positive??

Here's how the conversation went when the head of the department at the clinic entered the room with the Indian woman and me:

"Hi, how are you? Mr. Mitchell, is it?"

She was a short Asian woman with reading glasses sitting ever-so-condescendingly on the top of her head.

"Yes, ma'am."

"Okay, let's take a look at what we have here," she says with the glasses now sitting on the bridge of her nose.

"I see two lines. One is a bit faint. What does that mean?"

"Are you asking me, ma'am?" My catholic school manners had a way of shining through in excess whenever I became nervous.

"No, I'm talking to her." She looked over at the Indian woman. The Indian woman answered, "I'm not sure. One line is red, and the other is pink. So is it two lines or one?"

"There are two lines," the Asian woman exclaimed.

"What does it mean?"

"Well, one line means negative, and two makes it positive," the Indian woman answered. This went on for what seemed like forever until finally, the Asian woman became frustrated.

"I don't know how these tests go. I'm telling you that I see two lines. What does that mean?" The Asian woman had reached her capacity regarding this whole situation.

"It means it's positive," the Indian woman said. This time, her English was clear.

The Indian woman was sad now. I guess two HIV tests and some attempts at comforting me with stories of other people finding out they were HIV-positive while we waited made that Indian woman think we were friends.

And then it hit me. This wasn't like the other times. I felt like Samson in the Bible. You know, the guy with the great might because of his hair? No one could beat this dude. He was like, all-powerful. Well, when he was finally about to be defeated, and his enemies had him surrounded he thought, "I'll escape just like the other times and shake myself free."

There was no shaking HIV, though. It was mine to take home with me and anyplace else I went. I had spent so much time gambling with my health in the past that now it finally caught up to me. Just when I was doing well. Just when I was living right. Whether you believe in karma or your sin 'finding you out', sickness was so real in that moment. It stared me in the face in the form of a confused Indian woman and a stern Asian doctor. I have to hand it to that woman, though. She must have mustered up every ounce of sympathy in her tiny little body in order to look me in the eyes and say, "Well, this is what it is. We'll have to take blood to determine your viral load."

But like I said, that was four years ago, before I mastered the art of sneaking my pill in between bites whenever I wasn't alone for dinner. I had always feared that someone would ask me what it was for. "A blood condition," I would practice saying to myself whenever I ate alone. You know, just in case someone asked.

We pull up to the street that I live on, and Mr. Harris covers my face and rushes me through the crowd of reporters who have now camped out in front of my house. I fumble with my keys but eventually get us both inside.

"You got two minutes. Pack a quick bag and be back at this door. I'll wait for you."

I didn't think twice. Something about the way Mr. Harris had been taking care of me made me trust the sternness in his voice. So I run up to my room and pack everything I think I'll need for a trip that I'm not exactly sure about. Where does Mr. Harris want to take me?

Nonetheless, I grab the essentials:

Herschel backpack

deodorant

toothbrush and toothpaste

two t-shirts

handful of undies

handful of socks

handful of wife-beaters aka the male bra

cellphone charger

Complera bottle (for my uh, "blood condition")

I run back down to meet an anxious Mr. Harris at the door where I left him. "We're gonna pick up a friend up the block, and then we'll hit the road. You got everything you need?" he asks in a very concerned manner.

"That's hard to answer, seeing as how you haven't told me much about where we're even going," I answer sarcastically. "You'll be fine," he reassures me. Makes me wonder why he even asked in the first place. Nothing ever really worried me when I was with Mr. Harris. Something about his money and status makes me feel like there isn't a problem we'll ever run into that he can't fix.

Out we go. Back into the chaos and back under Mr. Harris' expensive suit jacket, which smelled of some expensive ass cologne that Justine told me is a mixture of three different colognes. Mr. Harris doesn't know that I'm aware of his irrational fear of becoming indistinguishable, even down to what he smelled like.

You never really know what it feels like to be a celebrity until everyone appears to be the same color through the tints of the window on a bulletproof Sprinter, and you're desperately tryna escape a crowd of reporters. We zip down Vernon Avenue and make two right turns that place us back on Myrtle Avenue. The Zombies hit Myrtle the hardest. Them niggas knocked down the Key Foods supermarket on Throop and the Cascade factory on Marcy. Cascade, man. Every Spanish kid I ever met growing up had a mom or aunt that worked at Cascade. Them shits have been leveled and have blue, wooden walls up to surround the demolition. What's most insulting is that those blue walls have pictures on them that show you what will be put up in place of what was knocked down. As if we give a shit about it.

The driver makes a sharp right onto Marcus Garvey Boulevard and stops on the corner of Vernon. There's a woman standing on the corner with a bag in her hand and anticipation on her face as if she had been expecting a ride. Our ride. And now I know this must be a joke because I've seen this woman before and there's no way in the world Mr. Harris knows her. No way she's coming with us to wherever the hell we're going.

"Mr. Harris, where are we going?" I ask as the woman boards the van and tosses her bag into the space next to my seat. Still smells of apples.

"That's not important," he assures me.

Great. We're going to an unimportant place with the White woman I interviewed in my shop just a few days ago.

This is gonna be fun.

10. **Confessions - Part I** (Usher)

When I was a kid, the Verrazano Bridge was something we would only ever pass under in order to get home from Coney Island. My dad would always tell us that there wasn't much on the other side of it except for Six Flags[16] and racist Italians. I had always thought that the Verrazano Bridge was prettier than the Brooklyn Bridge, even if all it led to was New Jersey. I'd never actually admit that to anyone though.

---

[16] Popular theme park where Lenny and Justine made out on a ride once. They never bring it up and no one else knows about it.

There's not a lot of traffic on our way over the bridge and into Jersey right now— probably because everyone else is on the other side of the medium trying to get into Brooklyn. I'm not allowed to have my phone. Mr. Harris took it away a few hours ago. I don't do too well with blind instruction, but part of me trusts Mr. Harris. Sara is here too, and she hasn't said a word.

"How do you know Mr. Harris," I ask her. She's sitting on my left, looking straight ahead as if she knows where we're going but isn't allowed to tell me. I keep sneaking looks at her but the Sun is shining through on her side of the van, and I can't tell how well she can see me, seeing her.

"We've worked together for years," she answers. "I know his driver too. Doesn't say much but that man is great with directions." Her bag is placed neatly in the middle-space between our seats.

"So I don't get it," I blurt out. "The whole interview for the job the other day- was that fake? What was that about?"

"I'll admit, the job interview was a means to an end. Mr. Harris had been in my ear about you for a while. He wanted me to go and challenge you. He expected you to do more for the community with the space you've been given. Believe it or not, he thinks pretty highly of you, and so I had to go and see for myself what all the fuss was about."

"And?" I ask eagerly.

"He was right," she says, through a smile. I can't help but smile too. Kinda makes me realize that I haven't smiled since Lisaura and I got reacquainted two nights ago. Jersey gets a bad rap, but it's got some pretty parts to it. The trick is to not get so caught up in all the power plants and nuclear waste.

I'm kidding.

I don't know if some of these are actually nuclear waste plants.

"So you're some type of counselor or something? Was that what you studied at Penn state?" I can't help but wonder if she's impressed that I remembered that from her résumé.

"You can say that," she responds.

"Well, you either are a counselor, or you're not. Which is it?"

"I tend to just be whatever the moment calls for, really," she says.

"Could you be a counselor right now?" I ask sarcastically.

"Is that what you need?" she replies in a more serious tone, almost as if to take me up on my offer. I think she might be serious.

"I guess," I reply. "Is this like Catholic school where I tell you my confessions?"

"It doesn't have to be that way," she assures me. "Why don't you just talk and I'll listen?"

Mr. Harris is in the front seat, looking out the window and humming along to something on the radio. I should feel weird about this whole situation, but I don't. No place is more uncomfortable than being back in that hospital room with Bree and being blamed for damn-near everything since slavery. Being in a van with a random White lady, Mr. Harris, and his silent driver is a dream right now. Even if I don't know where the hell we're going.

At first, the thought of opening up to Sara started to feel like one of those sessions they force you into in elementary school. I got sent to the counselor's office once to talk about why I wrote, "mommy" over and over again in my notebook during fourth period. I didn't wanna talk about it then with the weird, skinny guidance counselor who wouldn't let go of his obviously receding hairline. But now, at twenty-seven years old and with nothing left to lose, I figure I can afford to open up a bit.

It also dawns on me in this moment that no one that I know has ever asked me to talk while they listen. Not Justine, not Bree, not my dad, and definitely not Lisaura. I mean, Lisaura's sweet and all but even she seems to take up all the talking space in our relationship. I decide to let Sara have it. Plus, I wanna see how much this lady can handle.

"Okay," I finally say. "I'm down to talk but just know I'm not gonna clean this shit up. I've been through some pretty rough stuff."

"I'm not easily offended," she assures me.

"Okay," I say.

Big sigh.

"If I pulled out my dick, would you suck it?"

166

"Excuse me?" she asks with a shocked face.

"That's not me asking," I tell her. "That's what Travis Simmons asked me in the summer before seventh grade. I know what you're probably thinking: twelve years old is kinda old to be letting someone molest you, but I don't think it is. I mean, my cousin was thirteen when he first made me hump his sister under the covers without our underwear on, so where do you really draw the line? I was six, and she was seven. Ever since then, I kinda just let people do whatever they wanted to do to me, including Travis Simmons in 2002."

I take a break from staring at my fingers and look up to see if Sara has heard enough. Instead, she's staring right at me, waiting for me to continue. So I do.

"Travis Simmons came around way more than any of us could stand it. All I know is that Betsy from two blocks down had gotten a new batch of foster children and fifteen-year-old Travis was the newest addition that year. I'm sorry to call them 'batches' but it's true. That woman rotated foster kids like nobody's business. It was everyone's business though because the hood knew she was in it for the government checks and nothing more. But I guess Travis was cool because he was two years older. That nigga was annoying though- you okay with that word?" I ask to be sure I'm not offending her.

"I don't mind it. Keep going," she insists. So I do.

"Yeah so, Travis was always around. And I admit, I thought he was good-looking, but back then I wasn't sure if that was okay to think."

I look up again to check on Sara, and she seems to be doing okay still. If I'm being honest, I never talked about actually being attracted to Travis back then until just now. Sara didn't seem to mind, so I continue telling my story.

"Bree had caught my second abuser and me kissing just two years before me meeting Travis. It was a Saturday night when we were busted, and by Sunday morning my brother had informed my dad about what he saw. That Sunday morning in mass I watched my dad fight back tears through the entire service. When we got home he made me strip out of my clothes and without explanation, he had me lay across his bed so

168

he could beat me. Bree sat there on the bed and watched. I didn't expect him to say anything. His big brother had just been caught kissing his male cousin. I could never figure out if the whipping was because I was doing dirty things with my cousin or if it was because I was doing dirty things with a boy. There was no lesson. Just a beating. So a few years later, at twelve years old, I wasn't sure that Travis was such bad company."

"I'm sorry you had these things happen to you," Sara interrupts in a sweet voice. It actually sounds like she cares. "Will you tell me more about Travis? Did anyone ever catch you two? How did it end?"

"Um, I don't know how much more there is to say. I mean, I didn't think Travis liked me very much," I admit to her. "He preferred to hang with my brother and play video games with the other kids that lived in our brownstone. And that was fine with me because I was so used to being left alone. Being alone had become my thing. I could listen to my boombox with no interruptions. I was always busy trying to catch my favorite songs on the radio so that I could record them

169

on my Maxell tapes. That day, I didn't notice when Travis came in and shut the door behind him. Bree and his friends must've been in the living room, too caught up trying to figure out who had actually called 'next' for the game controller. That's when he asked me the infamous question from earlier," I tell her.

"If I pulled out my dick, would you suck it?" I repeat but not for shock factor, this time. This time, I just really need someone else to know how oral sex was introduced to me for the first time.

"Just like that, he broke the silence," I continue telling her. "I can't remember what was on the radio that day, but I remember staring straight ahead, almost paralyzed. It was the middle of the day, and Travis didn't need a ninja turtles sheet and a closet like my older cousin did back when I was six years old. Right there and then began my obsession with Travis Simmons."

"Obsession?" she asks in a confused tone.

"I'll explain," I assure her. "Nothing happened that day in my room. After the question that Travis so eloquently asked, I stared straight ahead and just shrugged my shoulders. And the truth was, I didn't know what I would do because the ones before him didn't ask. They just- 'did', you know? Travis planted something in me that day in my room. Almost like a drug addict's first hit. I mean, I have never been addicted to drugs, so perhaps that's an unfair analogy. But I guess hearing him ask that question was as if he was saying,

'In case you're interested, I'm here.'

It was almost permission. It was permission. So I sought him out one night. He wasn't so hard to find because he slept over EVERY night. Seriously, this kid hardly ever went home that summer. But I didn't mind, after a while. There were so many of us living in that brownstone back then so whenever it was the weekend, we all kinda fell asleep wherever sleep would find us. And although the top bunk was mine, I found a cozy spot next to Travis on the bottom bunk one night. I nestled in between him and the wall as if I had fallen asleep there like everyone else had fallen asleep: by 'accident'."

"It wasn't an accident," Sara states rhetorically.

"Of course not," I scoff. "As if I didn't notice that his groin was so near to my face that night. I didn't know what I wanted Travis to do but he seemed to want what the other molesters before him wanted. That night I guess I had a new answer to his question from the other day but isn't it like an abuser to make you feel like you want the abuse? I think so because that night I found comfort in between that wall and Travis on the bottom bunk. He refused me. In fact, I remember that he rolled over and fell asleep. Now that I think of it, he became frustrated that I found more comfort in just being there than actually doing anything. I guess I just enjoyed the attention from the cool kid that was three years older than me, who lived two blocks over. Attention wouldn't come free though. Not for long, anyways.

A few days after that, my dad and I were hanging out watching t.v. and Betsy knocked on our door, asking for a ride to run an errand. Betsy was one of the old geezers who were trying to get my dad to marry them because my mom wasn't in the picture."

"What happened to your mom?" Sara interrupts again.

"Shit, if I know," I say. "Anyway, my dad takes Betsy on her errand, right? And leaves me home alone with Travis until they got back. There was a nervousness that rose in me because I knew that the cat and mouse game between me and Travis would end that day. My dad and Betsy probably didn't even have their seat belts fastened completely before Travis began to chase me around the house. Bree was at the park with his friend Gabriel, and so it was just me and Travis. I avoided him until he agreed that watching TV would be a better idea than running around on the second floor. So we watched TV until Travis decided it'd be a great time to pull out his penis and pleasure himself. I hadn't seen someone else's penis up close since I was six years old. I guess they change a lot once you hit Travis' age. It took all of three seconds for me to realize I hated oral sex, so I jumped up and ran to the bathroom to spit. He didn't have an orgasm, so it wasn't semen that I tasted. I guess it was the taste of flesh that was so repulsive."

"Is that where it ended? Did someone find out?" Sara asks.

"Not quite. One day as he left to FINALLY go back home for a while, he asked me to walk him to the door. That day, in particular, he had done a great job at pretending that we were just friendly neighbors around everyone and secretly, that pissed me off. It's like at night; he would search for me, but during the day he'd make fun of me when everyone else was around. He started to disgust me. So I opened the door for him, and he walked out. He turned around before getting too far and said 'See you later.' And in one swift motion, as if there was no risk of being seen by anyone in my house, he kissed me. Me!"

"Why is that such a big deal?" she interrupts once more.

"Well," I continue, "I had always been the dark-skinned, fat, counter-sibling to my brother, Bree. On all the family outings when we partnered up, my cousins called dibs on being Bree's partner because he was cuter. But not this time. Not with Travis. He preferred me. And I know that sounds fucked up because he was a perverted freak but it felt good to be preferred for a change. Don't worry- nothing ever really happened between me and Travis. Nothing more than a few sessions of halfway attempts at an orgasm. Mostly for him. Actually, always for him.

The furthest we got happened once in the bathroom, with the door locked but that didn't go so well. He got upset when I didn't know what he was trying to get me to do. That day, Travis became the annoying kid from down the block again while we were in the bathroom and he finally gave up pushing. His reason for stopping being, 'you got shit on my dick'."

"Real smooth," Sara says sarcastically.

"Exactly," I agree. "He stopped coming around sometime soon after that. But he left a lasting impression. He left me with curiosity. In a way, I was glad he was gone. A few years after that, when I was a sophomore in high school, my dad was reading the newspaper as he normally would do in the mornings. He asked me if I remembered the name of the young kid who lived two blocks down and was always around. It had only been three years since I saw him, but I could never forget his name. 'Travis Simmons' I said with an intentional hesitation, as if I didn't instantly know who he was trying to get me to remember.

According to the newspaper article, Travis had become a little famous. He and his friends were headed to prison. Seems like whatever foster home he wound up in after being Betsy's foster kid led him to meet some girl. He and his friends were convicted of gang-raping that girl. 'That poor girl', I thought. It seemed like Travis lost the patience to ask anymore. The patience he showed with me."

"Wow," Sara responds. "And no one knows?" she asks.

"My girlfriend knows. My best friend Justine knows too," I say. Then I remember that Mr. Harris has been here the whole time. I look at his head, and it seems to be hanging low, slightly bobbing up and down. He's either asleep, and his body is being swayed by the motion of this van, or he's crying. I somewhat feel bad about how graphic I had been with Sara just now. Maybe I should not have been so explicit. Sure, that might have been uncomfortable to listen to, but she asked. And at least she wasn't me. At least she didn't have to live it.

"We're stopping for gas," Mr. Harris says in a groggy voice. He tried his best to cover that up just now, but I'm pretty sure he heard every word of my confessions.

11. Confessions - Part II (Usher)

"So you must really hate your brother," Sara insists.

"Hell no," I almost yell as I hold the door for her to get out. "Why would you even say that?" I ask, almost with an attitude now. Just when I was beginning to like this lady.

"I'm sorry," she admits. "I guess I just assumed you would resent him for telling your dad about catching you kissing your cousin when you were younger."

"It's not like that," I tell her. "Bree just didn't understand what was going on. I could never hate Bree. You know how sweet that kid is? We used to go to Jones Beach when we were kids, and he would leave his shirt on to get in the water so that I wasn't the only one. He knew I was insecure about being the fat kid and so he would never take his shirt off. We never talked about it, but I know that was the reason why. He's just thoughtful like that."

"So you two are close, yeah?"

"Do bears shit in the woods? Hell yes. Very close," I tell her.

Mr. Harris interrupts and asks if either of us wants something from the gas station. Sara declines, but I put in a quick request for a bag of Cheetos and an AriZona iced tea. The driver, whose name I am still unaware of is pumping gas, and it's only now that I begin to question whether or not he's an actual human. Seriously, this guy has not said one word. Only does what Mr. Harris says.

Sara and I spot a few benches off on the side, and both of us silently agree that it's a good place to post up for a sec. On the walk over to the benches, I notice she's not wearing any shoes. I think she's asking a question about Bree but I can't hear her because I'm disturbed as fuck by the fact that she's walking barefoot right now. We sit and then her words come into focus, kinda like when you yawn on a plane.

"Yes or no?" she asks, probably for the second or third time.

"I'm sorry," I blurt, with a shake of my head to come out of my daze. "What were you asking?"

"You and your brother," she repeats without frustration. "You'll be fine to make up because you two are so close?" she asks with a sure tone. I forgot he and I got into it yesterday. I mean, I didn't forget, but it left my mind for a while.

"Oh, we're fine," I tell her as if I'm sure. "We've definitely had worse arguments." The truth is that I don't know that he and I will be okay. At least not this time. Bree and I have had some falling outs, but I never know how strong our bond is until we make it through. We always make up in the most mundane ways. In 2012, we got into a fistfight when I came home from

180

college for Thanksgiving break. I forgot what it was about, I just remember Bree punching me in the balls to get himself out of a headlock I had him in. We also knocked the turkey off the table in front of the family. We stopped talking for weeks, and I thought that for sure, one of us was just gonna up and move across the country for good. One day, he called me while I was at school to say, "yo you good?" I replied, "yeah." And that was it. That's how we got good again.

"Good, then," she decided aloud.

"Yeah," I continue. "We're gonna be fine."

"You're not exhausted?" she asks.

"I am but the van is pretty comfy, so I'm good."

"No," she says. "I mean exhausted from carrying so much. You told me a story a few moments ago that involved at least three sexual abuse scenarios, you seem to have grown up with a chip on your shoulder about your mom being out of the picture, you mentioned a bit about insecurity regarding your body image, and you're basically playing 'dad' to your kid brother. You never talk to anyone about this?"

"Not really," I say. "Where I'm from, you don't get to be tired or talk about how bad you've got it. Cuz everybody's got it bad. Niggas just make it work, you know? Sorry for saying 'nigga' so much."

"Then don't say it," she suggests.

"Huh?"

"If you're gonna keep apologizing for saying 'nigga'- just don't say it," she explains.

"Did you just say 'nigga'?" I ask.

"So I can't say it?"

"Hell naw!" I tell her. "It's like, two women could call each other 'bitch' and it be a compliment, reaction, confirmation, and term of endearment, all in one. But if a guy said it? World War, for sure. You know why? Because it's all relational. And it's all relative. And it's subjective to the person using it. So yes, I could be a 'nigga', and my boys is my 'niggas', and my enemy is 'that nigga' but my sneaker connect is 'that. nigga.' and you, my friend, still would not be able to use the word- all while referring to you as 'nigga' if I wanted to."

"That's crazy," she admits.

"No," I say. "it's Black culture. I know it seems confusing or as if we change the rules as we go but that's just the way it is. Like, Bree's friend Gabriel- he's Puerto Rican. I'm talking, 'eats cheese crackers and café con leche for breakfast' Puerto Rican. He comes around, and he's always like, 'what's good my nigga?' and nobody really minds because he gets a pass. And reasonably so. Gabe was there for summer lunches at the public schools, and his mom traded food stamps for rent money like the rest of our parents did. He grew up in the shit so he can say it. But if a Puerto Rican dude that we didn't know came around and said it, it wouldn't fly. Cuz we don't know that nigga, feel me?"

"Not really," She admits.

"Right," I say. "And that's exactly why you can't say it."

Mr. Harris arrives almost just in time to save us from an awkward moment. For once, since I met her two days ago, I seemed to have finally schooled Sara about something and not the other way around. I didn't do it to be a dick. I just felt like she needed to know. Her face is different. Not offended. Enlightened. I don't think Mr. Harris can tell he stepped in right in time. Or maybe he can. Either way, he walks back over to the car and yells back at us that we're free to finish our conversation out here by the benches if we want. We take him up on the offer.

Sara is standing now. Not standing still, though. I think she's trying to process the 'nigga lesson' she just received because she's walking along the cement blocks that separate the gas station from the grassy, forest area. She's placing her steps one in front of the other, the way we used to do on the block as kids. I guess they do that where she's from too. It's not just a Black thing.

"So," she starts up while holding her arms straight out to keep her balance on the cement blocks. "There's gotta be something about your brother that you hate."

"Why you tryna get me to dog my brother?"

"I'm not," she insists. "I just know that you're not being honest about how you feel about your brother. And until you do, you're never gonna get from beneath all this pressure you're under."

184

"Who says I'm under pressure," I ask.

"Idunno, maybe that rant you so graciously went on in front of the world," she reminds me.

"That wasn't about Bree," I assure her.

"It was," she contests. "Where were you just moments before you went on that rant?"

"Upstairs with Bree," I say.

"Exactly. Something about him takes you over the edge, and you have to make peace with that."

"I am at peace," I tell her.

"You're not," she spews back. "But you'll get there. Just gotta stop taking the blame for everything. There's gotta be something Bree's guilty of, no?"

I see what she's doing here, and I'm not gonna let her have her way. I live this reverse psychology shit.

"You're tryna get me to talk bad about Bree in order to relieve my own stress," I tell her. "I see what you're doing."

"Not true," she says. "I'm trying to get you to be realistic about your capabilities. You really think you're in control of what's happening around you? Don't flatter yourself," she scoffs. "I'm trying to get you to be honest about what is actually your fault. If you're gonna beat down on yourself, at least let it be about stuff you're actually guilty of, right?"

She's right.

And I hate it.

"So," she continues with her arms still out like airplane wings. "What is Bree's fault? Where does he fall short?"

"Idunno," I begin to admit. "I guess he could be a bit more motivated about life. It just always makes me so mad that he's so smart and good-looking and innovative. Why can't he just make something of himself and get the fuck up outta Brooklyn, ya know?"

"Mhmm," she replies. She's in the grass now, stepping deep into the blades and clenching her toes around each bunch they come in contact with. "What else?" she asks, almost unsatisfied with the bit that I just disclosed.

"I guess he's a bit all over the place, too. He never feels one way for too long. He's sad and excited and depressed and enthused, all in one moment. He's got the ability to become these things altogether, and it

186

annoys me that you never really know what you'll get from him. Sorta like a time bomb," I say.

"What else," she demands. I hate how easily my walls come down with her.

"I hate that he's a dick sometimes. Not all the time but just sometimes. Like with my HIV. He's always making jokes and shit like it's not my real life. Like I'm not really sick with this shit."

"You're sick?" she asks.

Shit. I don't think I told her that already.

"Yeah," I say ashamedly.

She can tell.

"Don't be ashamed," she says in that caring tone like before, in the van when I told her about Travis Simmons.

"You sick too?" I ask boldly. Something about her tone tells me she knows what it's like. Not HIV but just something.

"Not anymore," she says.

"It's okay," I tell her. "We don't have to talk about it if you don't want to." She stops stepping around and sorta just stands on her tip-toes. She slowly lifts her blouse from her waist up and shows me a scar, just beneath her lower breast.

"Cancer?" I blurt out, probably in the most assuming and idiotic manner possible.

"That… and some other things," she admits with a smirk.

"What's so funny?" I ask.

"I beat it," she says with an even bigger smirk.

"Cancer?"

"All of it," she boasts.

"Must be nice," I say sarcastically.

"It doesn't have to be that way," she says as she steps toward me and back over the cement blocks to sit on the benches. Her feet are dirty and green with grass stains. I halfway covet her carefree demeanor. There's something that bothers me about seeing her barefoot in the grass. But what's a little dog-shit on the bottom of your feet after having beat Cancer? Almost makes me want to open up more about my illness except I'm upset that mine is still here and hers wasn't government-issued.

"What'd you mean just now?" I ask.

"What, about it not having to be that way?"

"Yeah," I say.

"Oh, I didn't mean to offend you. I just wonder why you're not better by now."

"Um, other than Magic Johnson, I'm pretty sure the rest of us are still waiting for the cure. Unless you know something I don't know," I tease.

"I get it," she says. "it's just not as hard as you think," she says while fidgeting with a blade of grass in her hands.

"The fuck are you even talking about?"

"Well," she says. "Do you want to be better?"

"Of course," I almost yell.

"Okay then," she says with a smirk.

"A cell phone!"

It was Mr. Harris, slow jogging to us with a worried look on his face.

"Are you asking for mine? Because you took it," I remind him with resentment in my tone.

"No, I'm talking about Bree," he says. "It wasn't a gun that he was holding. The footage is all over the news from the night he was shot. He was trying to show the officers his cellphone."

12. Interlude II (Lenny feat. Lisaura)

"It's not that I'm ashamed of you or anything. I just don't get why it's always gotta be a thing."

"A thing?"

"Not like that, Lenny. You know what I mean. It's just always a Black thing with you. The world is not out to get you. Not everything is about that. You know that, right?"

"Let's just drop it, Lee."

"Okay…. But you get what I mean right?
You don't always have to make a big deal about it
whenever something happens to Black people. It's like,
que no se meta en lo que no le importa, you know?"

"I said drop it, Lee"

"Okay. I'm sorry. It just makes it awkward for
everybody when you bring it up. That's all I'm saying.
Stick to easy topics like music and stuff. You don't have
to be Black Jesus all over Facebook."

"I feel you."

"Cool… Wanna go again?"

"Sure."

13. Hotline Bling (Drake)

"Can you believe it?" Justine yells. There's an excitement in her voice. She doesn't sound panicked like the last time we spoke. "It was a cell phone, Lenny! I knew everything was gonna be okay."

Will it be okay? I can't help but think that the video showing Bree with a cellphone and not a gun means that things will only get worse. Twitter will still be abuzz, hashtags have never been more useful, and car bumpers have never been more adamant about reminding you that the driver supports his or her local police enforcement. So, what does this mean? I don't share these thoughts with Justine. She can be in a bubble about things sometimes, and I don't always like to be the one that bursts it for her.

"That's great news, Justine. I'm glad."

"Glad? That's it?! Lenny, this means no jail time for us. We might even be able to sue!" Justine yells in excitement. I even have to pull the phone away from my ear because she's so loud. Maybe it's because we're back in the van and there's no outside noise to balance out Justine's volume.

"Where are you?" she asks.

"Idunno," I tell her. "Somewhere outside of Jersey, I think?"

"Jersey?"

"That's enough," Mr. Harris interrupts. He takes his phone back and tells Justine that we're fine. He reminds her that he loves her and that we'll be home soon. My phone is still being held captive, but I wish I had it. I would text Bree. Tell him that I'm sorry and that

I should've believed him all along. Mr. Harris hangs up, and I waste no time asking him a barrage of questions.

"Does this mean we're going back to Brooklyn? Is Bree okay? Where are these lawyers you were talking about?" Mr. Harris remains calm, and so does everyone else. Sara is back in her seat, and she seems to still be smiling, kinda like when you know somebody's business, but you promised you wouldn't tell anyone. Mr. Harris' driver is facing forward with his hands at ten and two. I have yet to hear him speak and I still don't know his name. He just keeps doing whatever Mr. Harris says. So in the same way we've been going, Mr. Harris leans over and whispers into his driver's ear. The driver nods his head and starts the engine.

"What's his deal?" I ask Sara.

"Whose deal?"

"The driver," I say. "Is he some type of silent monk or something?"

"Not really," she answers. "I think he's just good at taking direction."

"Yeah, but is he like paid to be silent or something? Why does he never speak?"

"He speaks," she says in a sure tone. "But he mostly just likes to do whatever Mr. Harris tells him to."

"Like a slave?" I ask.

"More like a servant," she retorts.

"You know where we goin'?" I ask.

"You'll see," she says.

There goes that smile again.

△ ▼ △ ▼

"Here you go," Mr. Harris says with his hand reaching back, over his headrest.

It's my phone.

"I can have it back?"

"Do you want it back?" he asks.

I don't know if I do. I don't know if I want to see pictures of the crime scene on Instagram or tweets about Bree. The sucky thing about social media is that it's not merciful. It's not respectful or forgiving. Because it doesn't have to be. Nothing can erase my stupid rant from the other night in front of all those reporters. There's no rule that could stop people from talking about Bree, even though they don't know him. I don't want to be me anymore. I don't want this to be us. I take the phone anyway.

I delete all my apps. Twitter, Facebook, Instagram- all of it. I put my text messages on 'Do Not Disturb' and I alter my settings so that it only allows calls and texts from one contact.

Bree.

So this way, if my phone goes off I'll know exactly who it is. I don't call or text him right away because it's pretty normal for me to try and make the peace. Instead, I decide that this time it's up to him. And that's pretty scary to do because Bree has taught himself how to live without people. It's why he's so good at ignoring Justine. It's why he insists that I'm wrong about the time I got snuffed for him in the park by P.S. 23 in 2001.

"You got snuffed <u>because</u> of me- not <u>for</u> me. There's a difference."

To me, there was not a difference. Bree had been bothering some kid at the park that day, and the kid went and got his older brother who had been in eighth grade. I was only in the sixth. The eighth-grader from the park didn't care that I was two grades below him. Somebody had to pay for making his little brother feel bad. My teeth are still chipped a bit from the punch I took to the jaw. I grabbed Bree's hand that day and we speed-walked all the way home. There was no stopping at Katy's candy store that afternoon after school. We weren't even supposed to be at the park. Bree didn't seem to care that my jaw was throbbing the whole way home. He had one concern as I gripped his hand tight, pulling his arm hard on purpose.

"You gonna tell dad what happened?"

"No, Bree. And neither will you!"

We pass a big blue sign, and it reads. 'Maryland Welcomes You: PLEASE DRIVE GENTLY'. We're going south. I don't know anyone from the south. Maybe we're going to one of Mr. Harris' houses. He's got plenty of them. Justine was always inviting me and Bree to one of their vacation spots over the summers. We always turned her down because my dad didn't want us freeloading off of her and her dad. Mostly, I think my dad was intimidated by the thought of someone else taking care of us better than he could.

Sara is awake now, and I catch her staring at me. I'm attracted to her but not like how I am with Lisaura. It's like, I like the way Sara makes me feel when she talks, but I don't wanna have sex with her. It's like I respect her; you know? She's like an older sister or a really smart aunt. She reaches her hand out across the space between our seats, and I grab it. It's warm and soft.

When we used to hold hands in Sunday school to pray, I had always made sure I was next to Yesseñia Jusino. She wasn't very pretty, and she bit her nails, but I liked holding her hand when the class prayed together. Yesseñia always readjusted her fingers to make sure our hands fit perfectly and when we all said 'amen' she would hold on for a few seconds more, even after everyone else had let go. That's how it felt to hold Sara's hand right now.

I can feel the van beginning to slow down now, and I can't remember when we began driving on a dirt road. Sara's hand is still firm in mine, and I think neither of us wants to let go. We pull into a driveway, but I don't think this is one of Mr. Harris' vacation homes. The house we just pulled into is pretty plain. It's not run-down or anything, but it's also not very special. I can't help but think that we could've driven out to Long Island to stay at a house like this.

People with bigger dreams would probably look right past this house, but I always dreamed of houses like this one. Bree and I call 'em Disney houses. You know, the ones where the mom has cooked this ginormous breakfast, and the kid rushes down, late for school. The kid kisses his mom with one piece of bacon in his hand and shouts back, 'gotta go, mom! I'm late for school!' Bree and I would trip out and wonder if White people really ran off to school leaving so much uneaten food on the table. Anyway, this house was like that. And I liked it a lot.

I look over at Sara, and she gives my hand a little squeeze, smiles, and nods just once. She doesn't break her stare, almost like she wants me to know that even after we separate our hands, she'll still want to be holding mine. I nod back because I feel the same way.

Mr. Harris slides back the door on my side and motions with his hand that I should step out. So I do. It's a sunny day in Maryland, which I guess isn't very strange for a September day. The driveway is smoothly paved, not like the dirt road on the way in. There's a basketball hoop at the end of the driveway, along with a few bikes. The closer I get to this house, the more I fall in love with it. The color, the grass around it, the roof—it's all perfect.

I turn around and realize that I'm the only one taking steps toward the house. Mr. Harris, his driver, and Sara are all three lined up with their backs against the van.

"Are we going in?" I ask with the Sun in my face.

"Not us," Sara says.

"Just you," said the driver. He finally spoke.

"But I ain't never been here," I shout back. "Whose house is this?"

Just then my phone rings.

That can only mean one thing.

"Hello?" I say enthusiastically.

"Go inside," Bree says.

"What? Bree, what's going on? Are you good?" I ask.

"I'm fine," he assures me. He doesn't sound like he did at the hospital. He sounds better. He sounds like it's an ordinary day.

"Come inside," he says. "We're waiting for you."

I look back, and the van is gone. I assume that my three travel buddies are gone too, and now my stomach is trying its hardest to escape through my butt again. The front door to the house begins to open, and I can't seem to activate my fight-or-flight instincts. Is there a 'freeze' instinct? I can't move, even as someone steps out of the house with a hand on their hip.

It's a woman.

And she looks just like Bree.

14. Stranger In My House (Tamia)

"We can talk inside, or we can walk around. The choice is yours." This woman was beautiful. She looks like she's about forty-maybe fifty (you know that Black don't crack). I know this woman. Or at least, I think I do. I've definitely seen her before. She's waiting for me to make up my mind.

"You know Mr. Harris?" I shout from the driveway.

"Better than you know," she shouts back. She reaches for something and then steps out of the house. Walking toward me, I can see that she grabbed a jacket.

"I guess we're walking, then," she says as she walks up to me. This woman is tall and beautiful. Her hair is thick and dark, like mine and her skin is smooth like Bree's. She's also got Bree's eyes. Or maybe he's got hers. I wanna ask her if she is who I suspect her to be but I honestly am trippin' the fuck out right now.

"Are you not gonna lock the door to your house?" I ask as she starts down the driveway without me.

"It's fine," she replies without looking back. "Besides, that's not my house. It's yours."

"Mine?" I yell as I slow-jog to catch up.

"Yep. Yours," she says, still looking forward.

Her arms are folded with her hands tucked underneath her biceps as if the September breeze is nipping at them. She's smiling big and taking in the sights around us. We're walking down a street with houses lined along the curb for as far out as I can see.

The houses are all different. Not one of them looks the same.

"Ready to see Bree?" she asks.

"Bree's here?" I ask enthusiastically.

"He's here," she says happily. "Well, he's here too, is what I should say."

"What do you mean?"

"Everyone you see today is actually here, but they are also where you last saw them."

"Everyone?" I ask with sarcasm and confusion in my voice.

"The best way for you to understand it is to loosen up your understanding of time. You were you yesterday, yes?"

"Yes?" I answer and ask at the same time.

"Exactly," she says. "Does that stop you from being you right now?"

"I guess not," I reply.

"There you go. The people here are exactly who you know them as, just at a different place in time."

"I think I understand. But what about Mr. Harris and his driver and Sara?"

"Oh, they're always dropping folks off here. But they're not always who they appear to be."

"What does that mean?" I ask.

"It means they tend to be whoever they need to be in order to get you here. They took the form of people that you would be most comfortable with."

The fuck was in those Cheetos?

"It's not the Cheetos," she says.

"How did you know-"

"Don't think about it too much," she interrupts. "So... Ready to see Bree?" she asks again.

"Yeah, of course," I say, realizing that my questions have been holding up the obvious agenda that this woman has planned for us.

"He's right over there." She's pointing at a house that looks just like the one we started walking from. The one that she said was mine. I can see Bree in the driveway, but he's younger. A lot younger. And he's having so much fun.

Without me.

"Bree!" I shout to him. He looks my way, and we both run to meet each other at the curb. As he runs closer, he grows taller, and his face gets more mature. Right before my eyes, he transforms into the Bree I know now. Twenty-six-year-old Bree.

"Wussup papi?" he asks as he meets me with a hug.

"Bree, where are we? What's going on?" I ask.

"It's fine Len. Didn't she explain it to you?"

"Yeah but- I'm so confused bro, what's going on? How'd you get here?" I ask.

"You're thinking too much pap, you just gotta let go."

"Let go of what?" I ask.

"Everything!" he shouts as he throws his arms out toward his sides. "It's bigger than Brooklyn and Zombies and you and me. You just gotta let it go. Even me," he says as he begins to shrink down again. He looks about six or seven years old now.

"I'm fine, Len. You don't have to worry about me! I'm fine." He runs back up the driveway, and I feel the woman behind me. I whip around with confusion on my face, and she's just there. Smiling.

"Ready to go?"

"Where now?" I ask.

"Justine is waiting."

The woman walks away without asking me to follow. I run to keep up with her again because it just seems like the right thing to do. I want to freak out but I can't. I don't know how to explain it, but there's no bad emotion when I'm around this lady. Like, seeing Bree just now made me sad, but I couldn't feel sad. Or even watching him transform right in front of me made me want to be afraid but I couldn't be. There's no fear or sadness here. Just peace and understanding.

"We're here," the woman says. I don't remember when it got to be so bright here, but I can hardly keep from squinting because everything seems to shine, even the streets. I can see lions and elephants at the curb in front of where we've stopped. I'm not surprised at all. We're at Justine's house.

Justine's house is small. It's like a hut almost, and where there was grass at my house, there seems to be dirt and shrubs at Justine's. I can see her in the doorway, and she waves for me to come in. I turn to look for the woman who brought me here, and she's there, standing with her arms crossed. She smiles and nods like Sara did in the van. She's gonna wait for me. I think that's what that means. So I go inside.

Justine's house is beautiful. In fact, it seems bigger inside than it appeared to be on the outside. No, I mean like way bigger. I sit at a table that is decorated with flowers and leaves, all colors that resemble autumn. Justine sits across from me, and she is beautiful. I mean, Justine has always been beautiful, but she's even more beautiful right now. Her skin is radiant like beads of sand on the clean beaches out near Long Island. Her hair is so long. I've never seen it so thick and lengthy. Even with it braided, it drags on the floor. I know this can't be my Justine because Justine fell off the stage in tenth grade during our fashion show rehearsal and split her eyebrow. She needed fourteen stitches, and the sew job was so bad that her skin healed over and created a scar where part of her brow didn't grow back. The Justine in front of me has a perfect brow. No scar. No missing hair.

"What is this place, Jus?"

"It's later," she replies.

"Justine, please don't be weird. I need you right now. Please help me. Tell me where I am," I beg her.

"You've always been, Lenny. And you'll continue on. Right now, you're here with me," she says.

"I don't know what that means."

"It means you've got work to do, Lenny. You have to open your mouth and speak for those who are being drowned out. The fight is difficult, but you hold the baton now. Don't drop it. Don't set it aside. Tuck it into your waistband and go!"

"Justine, what are you talking about?"

"The race, Len. You gotta run the race. I know it's hard, but you gotta keep going. You'll get it to the next person, and then they'll run, and then you'll rest. I know you want to quit, but your voice is more powerful than you think. Speak up and run tall. It won't hurt for long."

"I don't understand, Justine. Who am I speaking to? What am I running for?"

She grabs me by the hand and leads me to the doorway of an open room. The room has no floor, just a blank space.

"Look," Justine says. "What do you see?"

I peer down into the void where the floor should be, and the emptiness slowly appears to be a crowd. I can see the faces, and I recognize them all. They're teenagers from the block. Black kids, White kids, Spanish kids- I recognize them all. They're just standing there, waiting. A song comes on, and the crowd erupts into cheering and dancing. I know this song.

"Biggie?" I ask Justine.

"Which song?" she asks.

"Sounds like Hypnotize," I say.

"Exactly," she replies. "That's exactly it. Run for the hypnotized."

I know I said there are no bad feelings here but I think I was wrong. My eyes are hot and my vision is blurring. My heart feels like a thousand strings are tied around it and all the strings are being pulled at once. I blink so that I can see clearly again. The tears are warm against my face, and Justine reaches to wipe them away.

"What just happened?" I ask her.

"That's how He feels," she says.

"He, who?"

"It's time to go," she says as she leads me by the hand to the front door.

15. Alright (Kendrick Lamar)

It's still bright outside and Justine waves from
the door as I go back out to meet the strange woman
again on the street. She is exactly where I left her.
Arms crossed, leaning on one hip and waiting with
patience on her face. Only this time, she looks like her
eyes got hot and blurry too. I don't ask her if she had
been crying. We silently agree that she was.

214

"Who's next?" I ask to break the silence.

"Who said anybody was next?" she shoots back with a smile and a quick glance from the corner of her eye.

"Is there anybody else?" I ask.

"Do you want there to be?" she asks.

"I think the next person is you," I admit boldly. "I also think you're my mother but not really. I think you're the three people that brought me here but you're also you right now. And I know that doesn't make sense, but nothing has made sense from the moment I got here."

"Do you trust me?" she asks. She's turned to face me now. There's familiarity in her eyes, and although I want to cry again, I can't make myself sad or afraid enough to do so.

"There's none of that here," she says as if she heard my curiosity. "There's no sadness or sickness or racism or crooked cops or gentrification or any of the things that plague your mind."

"I don't want to go back," I tell her. "I don't want to pop pills to stay alive. I'm Black, and there's a target on my back. It's hard. It's way too hard. I can't figure

215

this sex shit out cuz too many lessons from too many people have confused the shit outta me. And I'm sick! Did you know I'm sick? I don't even know who gave it to me. How sad is that? And I can't handle being Bree's brother or dad or whatever. Where were you? Do you know that he's been shot? Do you know that I practically raised him? He's real fucked up in the head. He doesn't finish anything he starts. He's got OCD and is a complete mess, all at the same time. He does everything I do, and I'm afraid he'll never get it on his own. He's angry and hot-tempered, and he walks around with a lighter, burning down bridges as he goes along life, trying his best to love people. He doesn't know how. He hates women. And people think it's just Black women he hates but it's women in general. And it's because of you. It's cuz you left. You fucked him up. You left him to figure it out on his own, and now I'm here to tryna straighten out this whole thing." It all came out, kinda like it did in front of the hospital a few days ago.

"As if you could straighten anything out!" The woman shouts. "Do I have to speak your language?"

she asks angrily. Oh, 'what would Biggie say?' right? 'Stay far from timid'? 'Only make moves when your heart is in it'? Live the phrase, 'sky's the limit'[17]? Who do you think made the skies? Who do you think made Biggie? I made him notorious. I gave him that passion. I gave you that passion. I never left you. I'm the One Who kept you this whole time. You haven't even scratched the surface of what this is all about! Don't front like you don't know why I made you the way you are. Your shoulders are broad so that you can stand tall against opposition. Your heart is tender so that you give love freely. Your eyes, servile so that you don't look down on anyone. Your body, defective so that even when you do accomplish something impressive, you remember you're nothing without Me. You know Who I Am! And I know who you are. I brought you here, to Me. You were there, and now you are here. Look at you!"

I look to where she is pointing at, and I see my face in a mirror, perfectly placed before us. I'm shining, just like Justine a few moments ago. My clothes are all

---

17 *"Sky's the Limit" - 1997*

white, and I've never looked happier. My eyes seem to smile, and I recognize myself in this reflection. I envy the reflection and how clear my complexion is there.

Perhaps the most impressive thing in the mirror is the crown. It's golden and has beautifully colored stones in it. It rests on my high top fro. Not too high, like the Fresh Prince but high enough to remind the Zombies I was here first. I look back at the woman, knowing exactly who she is now. Or he is now. Maybe that's not important.

"You're royalty, kid. You are strong, and you are necessary. You are here with Me, but most importantly, I placed you there. Don't forget Who you came from."

I nod yes, and my eyes are hot again because I know that this means I can't stay. I know that it will be hard if I go back. I know that the world is ugly and unfair and that I am tired. But I know that it's alright because I am here. And if here is just later then I guess it's okay to go back to before. And sure, before sucks because Bree might not pull through, and Justine might never be enough, and some cops just gonna keep being crooked, and Lisaura might not ever understand why it sucks to be Black in America. Even with all these things, I have a feeling that we gon' be alright.

A wooden box appears before us, and the door swings open slowly. The box is empty and dark; so dark that I can't see the back of the box by looking in. This box is tall, like me, and wide enough for a person to lay inside of it like a coffin.

"You trust me?" she asks again. I want to say yes, but I'm afraid of what that answer means.

"Get in."

I don't want to, but I do. A smile on the face of my mother is the last thing I see before the door closes and I lay in complete darkness. I'm crying now, even though I don't really know what for. The box is falling, and I can feel that it's falling pretty quickly. I think I've landed on something, but the impact was not hard at all. There is darkness still, and I'm afraid to push open the door.

It's quiet, but I hear something.

Glass.

Something is hitting glass.

Like a window.

A window!

Someone's throwing rocks at a window!

I push with all my might and what initially feels like pushing a heavy door becomes light like a bed-sheet as the Sun breaks in and my hands are up against my covers.

I'm in bed.

Rocks are being thrown at my window.

In 2017, someone is throwing rocks at my friggin' window. I check my phone, and it's 8:17 in the morning.

It's Saturday.

Alexis!

The shop!

I open the window and yell to Alexis that I'll be down in just a few minutes.

I'm confused.

Biggie would say it was all a dream[18].

But this was bigger than a dream. Maybe I'll meet a woman named Sara today. Maybe she'll

---

[18] *"Juicy" - 1994*

challenge me about not being a louder voice in this community. Or maybe she'll just be a girl looking for a job at a coffee shop. All that I'm sure about is that Lisaura is mad about something Bree posted on Facebook the other day. And the last time I saw Bree, we were parting ways at the bottom of the steps. I lean over and see the clothes I peeled out of after I picked Bree up from the station last night.

I grab my phone again.

Me: You downstairs?

Baby Bro: Yeah.

Me: Alright.

"So let me get this straight. You had a dream that I got shot and that Justine's dad took you to heaven with a White girl? Haha! Nigga, you buggin'.'"

I'm standing in his doorway and Bree is 100% convinced that I'm crazy. Or that one of the side effects of my pill is what caused me to see what I saw. But I know what I saw, and it was hardly a dream. I wish Justine was here. She would see things my way.

"It wasn't a dream," I tell him. "It was like a vision. And it was really real, Bree. I promise you that I felt it. The anxiety of thinking you might be dead, the fear of not having you here, the look on our mother's face-"

"Oh, right," Bree interrupts. "You saw our mother, except she was God and she gave you advice about saving the world and fixing racism." He's rolling his head around and making his eyes go to the back of his head as if to mock me while he says all of this. "Wait! And our mother, who was also God, spoke to you in Biggie lyrics?" He throws his head back and laughs some more.

I'm frustrated that he won't at least try and understand. This is one of those moments when I hate Bree. Why's he always gotta make fun of things? As if I'm not late for work right now. As if I won't see Officer James or my dad today without having to make sense of the way they appeared in my vision. "When you say it like that it sounds weird but yes," I tell him, "I guess that's what happened."

"Then how you gonna change the world, Dr. King? Cuz from where I'm sitting, you still ain't got no girl— and that's kinda my fault. That's my bad. But yeah, you still ain't got no girl, the cops are still out here killing niggas and there still ain't a cure for that shit you got going on in your blood. So, welcome back to reality, bruh. Ain't nobody rockin' crowns down here. This is how we livin' on the other side of that weird ass vision you had last night."

Bree's right. And I'm not upset at his outlook on life because he always tends to be more Malcolm than Martin. Whether it was a vision or a dream or whatever, my life is still pretty fucked. And the truth is, I don't really know what to do about it. Real or not, I had an experience that helped me understand just how much of my past I have not dealt with.

Here's what's real: when I was six years old, I was molested. And again when I was ten. And again when I was twelve. At age twenty-three I was diagnosed with HIV, and it caused me to withdraw from life. I became stagnant. Much like my sexual abuse, I let my diagnosis take the driver's seat, and I allowed life to just have its way with me. I've got a knucklehead brother that I love and hate, all at the same time. The woman I love thinks that racism is dead and that discrimination in America doesn't affect her because she's Hispanic. My dad has decided that this brownstone in the hood is all his life will ever amount to, and there's a chance that Brooklyn isn't even where my anthropology begins. As much as I love Brooklyn, it really don't give a shit about me.

If I'm being honest, I'm pretty sure I met God last night. But I don't even know who to ask about that because the preachers around here drive Benzes and all they worried about is you sowing a seed. And if I am really losing my shit the way Bree is suggesting, then I blame it on the pressures of life. I blame it on not being able to cry out for help without being labeled an extremist or over-exaggerator. I blame it on being forced into a game where it's already been decided that people like me don't win.

It may not make sense to you, but this is really how it is where I'm from. And maybe you can't relate but don't ever say nobody told you. After all, what would Biggie say?

'If you don't know- now you know, nigga...'

Acknowledgements

Man, this book would not exist without the culture. But how does one thank the culture? Do you start with Hype Williams, for turning the soundtrack of my childhood into visual snippets of straight-up GENIUS? There's not enough paper in the world to do it. So I'll give a special thanks to my mom for doing her best with six kids in a four-bedroom Brooklyn apartment. Special thanks to my siblings, who taught me what friendship and loyalty mean. To Paul Reese, who showed me the unconditional love of a father but is indeed a robot, through, and through. To men like Dr. Bill Hackett and my pastor, Jason Burns, who taught me that it's okay to tell my story the way it is and that it actually matters to the world that I tell it. To my loving wife who is patient, and kind, and forgiving, and way too good for me- thank you, especially for believing I could even write a book in the first place. To friends like Tara, and Jason & Hillary DeMeo, who would not let me get away with disqualifying myself from living out a dream! To friends like Anastasia, Lis, and Mina, who took so much time to walk me through putting together something wonderful- thanks a lot, ladies. TO DEREK FOREHAND WHO SLAYED THE IN-DESIGN SESSION OF THIS BOOK IN EXCHANGE FOR A $5 STARBUCKS DRINK- THANK YOOUUUUU! And to Gabe Reyes for assisting with perfecting the re-release because I'll draw it but I won't ever learn to outline in Illustrator. To every Lisaura that has ever had to deal with the Lenny in me- thank you for your patience and sacrifice. Special thanks to a woman named Pepsi, who relentlessly shared the Gospel with me and wasn't put off by a Brooklyn boy who called her crying one morning after having a God-sized dream. To Ernie, and Nathan, and Morgan, and everyone else who read thousands of versions of this story- thank you for grasping my vision and encouraging me through it all. I'm eternally thankful for God and His relentless pursuit of my heart, and soul, and mind. Interestingly enough, Donald Trump taught me that people will look past obscene language if the story is good enough. So..

thank you? Meh…. I guess the biggest 'thanks' goes to you- the reader. However this book might have made it into your hands, I appreciate that you took the time to read it. If you enjoyed the ride that 'Bro.' took you on, I hope you're ready for many more trips through this crazy mind of mine.

God bless!

-Gregory M. Francis

A Very Special Thank You

Although this book borrows a lot from the people I know and love in order to create the world it takes place in, the one aspect that words on pages could never capture is the person who truly inspired this book: My brother and very best friend,

DaShawn Francis.

Man, the chapters of our real lives have been crazy. But don't we always get it right? Eventually? I'm so glad I never had to go too far to find my best friend. We had outside folks come and go, but our thing is what's really lasting, ain't it? I admittedly didn't get this part right the first time. But if we going off 'first times', there wouldn't be no times, amirite?

Thank you for always forgiving me. Thank you for being my hardest critic and my biggest champion. Thank you for using your voice to fight for me in the times when I was afraid to use my own.

This book ain't called 'Bro.' For no reason. Nigga, you it! But if I gotta actually say it, that's not a problem either. I love you, kid. You know it. The fam knows it. And if this book does well enough, the whole world will know it. I mean it like it's the first time, every time.

Thank you.

Q&A with Greg Francis and readers.

Why Bro.?

I wrote this book for a few reasons. The relationship Lenny and Bree have is closely based on the relationship I have with my brother in real life. I wanted to write a story that people would love but one that was also true. I figured that if I could get people to love the characters, then they would also love what the characters love. The spin is that the characters are real and so is the world they live in. It's a lot harder to hate people when you really know them. Mostly, I wanted people to get a closer look into the psyche of Black people and why we often think, speak and act the way we do.

Why the curses if you're Christian?

I truly believe God wanted me to tell this story in its most raw and true form. The saddest thing about a testimony is when it is edited and cleaned up before God even arrives on the scene. Where's the glory in that? Nothing in this book was added for shock factor. It's all real and it's happening in the homes of the families that sit in our churches. What's worse is that when we don't tell these kinds of stories, we become removed, or worse- repulsed by the very people that God wants us to love and understand.

Why such a crude ending?

More than anything, I wanted to write a book that would call the reader to action. A happy resolve where all of the characters live happily ever after just is not realistic. The truth is, the issues mentioned in this book are still prevalent and don't seem to have real resolve. I hope that the reader would put this book down, call up a neighbor and ask questions. Dialogue. Seek to understand. So you know a Lenny? Call him and remind him of his worth. Perhaps you know a Justine. Text her and remind her that 'Black' does not mean "less than" and that her confidence is not offensive. Meet an Officer James for coffee. Pay for the drinks and ask him what it's like to suit up and put himself in the line of fire every day when cops are at an all-time "hated" high. This is nothing new. Other writers have invoked deeper thoughts than I. I'm just running my race at the time I've been placed in.

Will there be a "Sis."?

Haha! Maybe... If it comes to me. If it becomes necessary for me to write. If it begins to break my heart the way the idea for 'Bro.' did. I love women so much. I'm in awe of what they're made of and what they're capable of and it's such a shame the way this world disregards the value of a woman. I've got a few friends with stories that would blow you away. I think there might be a time when we see 'Sis.' in our Amazon carts.

The n-word is such a touchy topic. Can you talk more about why you used it in the book?

The word 'nigga' is arguably as important as the word 'yo' to the hip-hop culture. It has seen more changes than P. Diddy's name. At first, it was this term intended to harm the person on the other end of it. Then the hip-hop culture adopted it and made it interchangeable. It could stand in place of any pronoun, insult, or even term of endearment. Currently, it can be found in music, movies, or even a fight video on Youtube. I think that the hip-hop culture has (knowingly or unknowingly) permitted this upcoming generation to use the word with no real consideration of its origin. No one really knows where the culture stands as a collective about who "can and can't use it" anymore. The word, much like the other colorful words in this book, was important to include because it's authentic to the world that these characters live in. The story would not have been real without it.

The Confessions chapter was a bit intense. Was that necessary?

Absolutely. 100%. Without a single doubt, it is always important to talk about the realities of sexual abuse and the stigma that comes with it. Sadly, this is one of the chapters that is closer to my reality than I would like. Sexual abuse is so real, and so prevalent in minority families, and so damaging. We don't talk about it enough. There's such shame and guilt attached to it and when it isn't dealt with and processed correctly, a victim can live a life in complete response to what happened to them. I hope to have every person who's ever been abused that way to know that it's okay to talk about it and that there is life and healing on the other side of such an ugly reality. If it was uncomfortable reading about it- good. Allow that discomfort to drive you toward reaching out and loving someone who's been abused.

HIV. Talk about it.

It sucks. It's real but it's not the same HIV that we saw when it first arrived on the scene in the 80s and 90s. It's no longer a death sentence but it's certainly a life sentence. I pray every day that a cure is something I see in my lifetime. The saddest thing I ever learned about HIV is that some men and women never get it under control because they don't have the love and support they need to believe they can be healthy. It's not easy receiving such a diagnosis. I wanted poz readers to see that HIV is manageable and that life does not stop at the diagnosis.

What's up with the crown?

It's simple. We're royalty. All of us. We can get caught up in our insecurities and shortcomings OR we can take those things and find purpose in them. Lenny's revelation is for all of us. In good times and bad, we're still valuable. And we're still purposeful. Sometimes we think the things we've been through are the things that can disqualify us from being able to put in work. It's quite the opposite. The things we've been through are the things that validate us! I can speak on these things because they are my reality. Who can tell me otherwise?

What now?

More books. Maybe some film? A series (Holla at me, Netflix, and Hulu). Seriously, though. I just want to create experiences that people can see themselves in so that they might identify the reason for their story. One of the most freeing experiences for me was when I realized exactly who I was and why I was made to be the way I am. If we can all tap into that, imagine how we might coexist. Imagine the force behind a confident, healing, and loving generation? Pshtt...

www.ingramcontent.com/pod-product-compliance
Lightning Source LLC
Chambersburg PA
CBHW022204170626
46807CB00005B/2340